Key Lime Murder

A COZY MYSTERY

KYLA HARRIS

This is a work of fiction. Names, characters, places, events, and organizations are the products of the author's imagination or are used fictitiously. Any resemblance to actual persons, live or dead, businesses, events, locales, or organizations is entirely coincidental.

Text copyright © 2024 by C.H. PRESS
All rights reserved.
No part of this book may be reproduced, copied, or transmitted in any form or by any means, without direct written permission from the author or the publisher. The only exception is for brief quotations used in reviews or promotions.

Chapter 1

Monday

The aroma of freshly baked key lime pies filled the air as I moved swiftly around my bakery, "Sara's Sweets." The line of eager customers stretched out the door, and the soft hum of conversation blended with the sound of the cash register.

"Next in line, please," I called out with a warm smile.

"Hi, Sara! Can I have two slices of key lime pie, please?" asked Mrs. Thompson, one of my regulars.

"Of course, Mrs. Thompson. How's your granddaughter doing?" I carefully packaged her order.

"She's preparing for her final exams. You know, she can't get enough of your pies," Mrs. Thompson said with a chuckle.

"Well, I'm glad she enjoys them." I handed over the package.

Directly in front of me, the large glass display case was like a treasure chest. Rows of flaky pastries, decadent cakes, and, prominently, my signature key lime pies with their tempting, creamy green filling.

In the cozy seating area to the left, wooden chairs were pulled up to tables covered in checkered tablecloths. The bookshelves along the walls, filled with cookbooks and mystery novels, invited customers to linger over their coffee.

The right side of the bakery housed our beloved espresso machine. The bakery's pastel-colored walls, adorned with framed photos, radiated a warmth that seemed to embrace each visitor.

This little corner of Key West, Florida had become my home, and every day I poured my heart and soul into creating delicious treats.

I was arranging a tray of almond croissants when Madison, my younger sister and one of my three employees at the bakery, emerged from the kitchen, balancing a tray of freshly baked key lime pies. The aroma was a blend of zesty lime and sweet, buttery crust that immediately made my mouth water.

"Careful with those, Maddy," I said, as she maneuvered the large tray onto the display case.

Madison flashed a grin. "Don't worry, Queen Bee, I've got this."

"These look amazing," I complimented. "You've outdone yourself this time."

Madison's smile widened, as she carefully placed a "Freshly Baked!" sign next to the pies. "I tried a new technique for the meringue topping."

"I'm sure they'll be gone before noon."

With the morning rush starting to calm down, I turned my attention to the next batch of key lime pies. In the kitchen, I measured each ingredient, ensuring the perfect balance for the pie filling. My fingertips danced across the countertop as I mixed the dough, feeling the satisfying smoothness that came with just the right consistency.

A familiar voice broke the silence, "Watcha making, Sara?" I looked up and saw Tom, my husband. His rugged appearance, with short, curly hair and a strong build, was only softened by the warmth in his eyes. The gleaming firefighter badge on his uniform caught the light as he moved closer.

"Another batch of key lime pies, of course. How was your shift?"

"Long, but nothing too crazy, thankfully." Tom just finished a 24-hour shift. He leaned against the counter. "How's business?"

"Booming," I responded with a wink, continuing to mix the dough.

"Hey, when are you planning on taking a break? I was looking forward to having some time alone with you in the back office," he said eagerly.

I paused to look at Tom's blushing cheeks and felt a tingling sensation in my stomach. "Just give me 30 minutes," I said softly, tucking away a stray strand of hair from my forehead.

Madison stepped between Tom and me, placing her hands on her hips. "You two, go find a room," she said with a playful wink.

Tom smiled at her and said, "Maddy, don't you have work to do? Customers to serve?"

I simply shook my head at their banter.

"Speaking of work," Madison said, "I need some help unloading flour from the truck and moving it to the storage room. Any volunteers?"

"It would be my pleasure," Tom offered, accompanying Madison out the back door toward the parking lot.

"Mommy!" Amanda burst through the back door, her cheeks flushed with excitement.

Ava, my dear friend, followed Amanda through the door. She had just picked up Amanda from daycare.

"Thank you for picking her up," I said to Ava.

"Don't thank me. Now, where's that delicious key lime pie you promised?"

I pointed toward a table nearby. "Over there. It just came out of the oven an hour ago."

"I have to run. I have a yoga class to teach in 20 minutes," Ava said as she grabbed the pie and headed toward the door.

"See you tomorrow at lunch!" I called after her.

Ava gave a quick wave goodbye before nearly colliding with Tom at the door.

"Hi, sweetheart," Tom greeted Amanda, reaching out to ruffle her hair affectionately. "Mom's just finishing up a batch of pies. Why don't you take a seat and show me that masterpiece of yours?"

"Okay, daddy!" Amanda exclaimed, jumping onto one of the stools and eagerly unfurling her artwork.

"Alright, these pies are ready for the oven," I announced proudly, sliding the tray into the preheated oven.

I turned to see Amanda selecting colored pencils from her pencil case. She was working on a new drawing. Her bright blue eyes were focused on her artwork, and her tongue peeked out of the corner of her mouth in concentration.

"Mommy, can you help me pick a color for the flowers?"

"Of course, sweetheart." I wiped my hands on my apron before joining her at the small table near the window. "How about we use this shade of pink?"

"Ooh, I like that one!" Amanda grabbed the pencil and added vibrant petals to her drawing.

Just then, Ginger, our border collie, trotted over to us, her reddish-brown tail wagging. She nudged my leg with her wet nose, seeking attention.

"Hi, girl," I murmured.

As the bakery door chimed, signaling the arrival of a new customer, Ginger's ears perked up. I walked to the front counter and greeted the woman with a warm smile.

"Welcome to Sara's Sweets! How can I help you today?"

"Hi there!" She beamed back at me. "I've heard so much about your key lime pies. Can you tell me what makes them so special?"

"Of course! As you may know, the secret to a perfect key lime pie lies in the freshness of the ingredients, especially the key limes. We make sure to use only the freshest key limes sourced from local growers. That's what gives our pies their zesty flavor and aroma."

"You must love baking to put so much thought into each pie."

"I do," I admitted, taking a pie out of the display case to show her.

The late afternoon sun cast a warm glow on the bakery's vibrant walls as I prepared to close up for the day.

"Mom, look!" Amanda proudly held up a drawing of our family. "Can we hang this one on the wall?"

"Absolutely, sweetheart."

As the last customer exited the bakery, Tom entered. "Ready to call it a day?" He wrapped his strong arms around me in a comforting embrace.

"Yes." I leaned into his warmth.

As the bakery's "closed" sign was flipped, an email notification chimed from my laptop in the office. Flicking through the unread mails, my heart plummeted as I saw the name "Maxwell Lee." He was a food critic, infamous for his harsh reviews that could make or break a restaurant. And he had decided to visit my bakery.

I sighed and shared the news with Tom, who was busy cleaning the espresso machine. He shrugged it off. "Sara, your pie is sure to impress him."

"I hope so."

Together, we locked up the bakery and stepped out into the cool evening air. In the distance, I could hear the faint cawing of seagulls and the gentle lapping of waves against the shore. A soft breeze blew through my hair, carrying with it the salty scent of the ocean. Ginger wagged her tail excitedly as she followed at our heels.

"Mom, can we have key lime pie for dessert tonight?" Amanda asked.

"Of course."

That night, I lay in bed, unable to sleep. The thought of Maxwell Lee coming to the bakery brought a shadow.

Chapter 2

Tuesday

The morning sun bathed the bakery in a warm glow as I wiped down the counters and checked on the ovens. The scent of buttery crusts and key limes filled the air, welcoming customers with the promise of delicious treats.

"Evelyn, have you tried our new chocolate ganache cake?" I asked one of my regulars, who had a sweet tooth.

"Chocolate ganache, you say?" Evelyn's eyes lit up. "Well, I might have to try a slice of that along with my usual key lime pie!"

"Coming right up!" I placed a generous slice of cake and a perfectly golden key lime pie on a plate for her.

The bell above the door chimed as another customer entered. I recognized him immediately— Maxwell Lee, the notoriously harsh food critic. In his forties, he was a tall and lean figure, with slicked-back hair and a perfectly fitted suit that oozed confidence and superiority.

Clutching my apron, I mustered a smile and approached him.

"Mr. Lee, welcome to my bakery. Please, have a seat at your table of choice."

He surveyed the room with a critical eye before choosing a table near the window.

"Mr. Lee, what can I get for you today?" I tried to gauge his mood.

"I've heard a lot about your key lime pie," he replied, a smirk on his lips. "I'd like a slice."

"Sure," I nodded quickly and rushed to the kitchen to make his order. Antonio, my employee for the morning shift, and the other customers watched in hushed anticipation.

Returning to the dining area, I placed a plate with a perfectly sliced piece of key lime pie in front of Maxwell. The vibrant green filling contrasted beautifully with the golden crust, a dollop of freshly whipped cream sitting atop like a fluffy cloud.

"I hope you enjoy our key lime pie, Mr. Lee."

He nodded and took a small bite. Time seemed to stand still as he chewed slowly. A heavy silence filled the bakery as all eyes were fixed on the critic. Then, setting down his fork, he looked up sharply, his face contorted in displeasure. "This is far too sweet, Sara. A key lime pie should be tart, a dance of flavors on the tongue. This is a misstep."

I felt a surge of defensiveness. "I respect your opinion, Mr. Lee, but my key lime pie is a balance of flavors. It's not just about the tartness; it's about the harmony between sweet and sour."

"Harmony? No, Sara, a key lime pie must highlight the key lime's natural zest. What you have here is a dessert for those who fear the true essence of lime," he retorted dismissively.

Feeling my cheeks flush, I took a deep breath. "With all due respect, Mr. Lee, my customers love this pie. It's not just about following a traditional recipe; it's about crafting a taste that resonates with my customers."

Lee leaned back, scrutinizing me. "A true culinary artist knows the importance of authenticity. You've catered to the masses at the expense of the art."

My hands clenched at my sides, but I maintained my composure. "Baking is an art, and like all art, it evolves. My key lime pie is slightly sweeter than traditional recipes, yes, but it's also rich and tangy."

He sighed, a hint of frustration in his gaze. "You're missing the fundamental elements of the pie. It's a culinary misstep."

"Our disagreement seems to be a matter of personal taste, Mr. Lee." I stood my ground.

"A matter of personal taste?" He raised his voice, causing a few heads to turn in our direction. "No, it's a matter of culinary principle. You've drowned the key lime's zest in sugar."

Maxwell stood up abruptly, his chair scraping against the floor. "This is not what a key lime pie should be!" His face was now a deep shade of red.

"I'm sorry, Mr. Lee. I didn't mean for this to become such a heated discussion." Without another word, I retreated to the sanctuary of my kitchen, feeling a mix of frustration and worries.

A glance at my phone reminded me that I was running late for lunch with my friends. In a hurry, I rushed out the back door and toward my car.

Chapter 3

I pushed open the door of "The Cozy Corner" and spotted Ava, Jennifer, and Sophia at our usual table.

"Sorry, I'm late, everyone," I apologized, removing my apron and tucking it into my bag.

Ava waved off my apology. "No worries, Sara! We've just been catching up."

Jennifer, the dependable accountant, offered a sympathetic nod. "We know how busy the bakery gets. How's everything?"

Sophia, who balanced her bossy lawyer persona with a touch of humor, chimed in, "Yes, sit down before I file a motion for tardiness!"

I chuckled and slid into the booth. The aroma of fresh coffee and the day's specials wafted from the kitchen.

"The morning rush was insane today."

Ava leaned forward. "Any interesting customers today? You always have the best stories."

I grinned. "You wouldn't believe me if I told you. But first, let's order."

The waitress came over to take our orders. We each fell into our usual choices—Ava with her health-conscious salad, Jennifer opting for the soup and sandwich combo, Sophia choosing the day's special, and me, craving the comfort of their famous chicken pot pie.

"So, Maxwell Lee visited my bakery this morning. He thinks my key lime pie was too sweet." I played with the edge of my napkin, feeling the weight of the critic's harsh words.

Ava reached across the table. "Sara, don't let one person's opinion get you down. Your pies are the talk of the town!"

Jennifer chimed in, "Exactly. You can't please everyone all the time. Besides, I've never heard anyone else complain about your pies."

Sophia spoke with conviction. "Maxwell Lee is known for being overly critical. Don't let his comments undermine your confidence."

"Do you guys think my key lime pies are alright? Be honest, are they too sweet?"

Ava laughed softly. "Sara, your key lime pie is perfect. It's got that ideal balance of sweet and tart. I always look forward to it after my yoga classes."

"And as someone who appreciates the finer things in life, I can assure you, your pies are nothing short of perfection," Sophia added.

Jennifer nodded in agreement. "I've crunched the numbers, and if sales are any indication, your pies are a hit."

Sophia, sipping her coffee, set her cup down with a clink. "You know, Maxwell Lee's reviews can be devastating. Just last year, 'The Rustic Table' closed down after his negative critique."

Her words sent a shiver down my spine. The thought of "Sara's Sweets" suffering a similar fate was unthinkable.

"I'm really worried. What if his comments turn customers away? My bakery is everything to me."

"Sara, your bakery is a staple in this town. People love your creations, especially your key lime pie. One critic's opinion won't change that," Ava said.

Jennifer nodded. "Exactly. You have a loyal customer base. And remember, not everyone agrees with Maxwell Lee. Forget about what he said."

Sophia leaned forward, her eyes earnest. "And let's not forget, 'The Rustic Table' had other issues. It wasn't just Lee's review. You run a tight ship, Sara. Your bakery will be fine."

Their words began to ease the knot of worry in my stomach.

"You're right," I said. "I can't let one critic's opinion overshadow all the positive feedback I've received over the years. Maxwell enjoys the tangy and refreshing taste of key lime pies, while I prefer a smoother and more aromatic recipe."

"That's the spirit!" Ava exclaimed.

Chapter 4

Returning from lunch with a lighter heart, I pushed open the door to "Sara's Sweets." The bakery was quieter than usual. I was about to head behind the counter when something in the corner caught my eye.

There, in a secluded spot by the bookshelves, lay Maxwell Lee. His eyes stared blankly at the ceiling. My initial thought was that he was merely resting, but something about his stillness sent a shiver down my spine. I approached cautiously, my heart pounding in my ears.

"Mr. Lee?" I called softly, but there was no response. Kneeling beside him, I realized with a jolt of horror that he was not breathing. His face, so animated in argument this morning, was now unnervingly serene. I reached out a trembling hand to check for a pulse, but there was none. *Maxwell Lee was dead.*

Could our argument have led to this? The thought sent a chill down my back. Heart attacks weren't unheard of in moments of high stress, and Maxwell might have pushed himself too far. Guilt gnawed at me, the weight of our heated exchange heavy in my chest.

I looked around, half expecting to find a clue, a sign, anything that could explain what happened. But there was nothing out of the ordinary—just the usual tables and chairs, the counter displaying an array of pastries, and the espresso machine humming softly in the background.

My mind raced with confusion and fear. What should I do? Who should I call first? The police? An ambulance? My thoughts were a whirlwind of shock and disbelief.

Gathering my wits, I rushed to the bakery's phone, my hands shaking as I dialed 911. "Please, come quickly," I stammered to the operator. "There's a man... He's dead. He's in my bakery."

As I waited for help to arrive, my bakery, once a haven of warmth and sweetness, felt cold and alien. The cheerful chime of the bell as customers entered and left seemed distant, surreal. I stood there, numb and trembling, my eyes fixed on the still figure of the once formidable food critic. His eyes were wide open, glassy, and unseeing. There was no mistaking the terror etched into his pale face.

It was then that Madison rushed over. Her eyes widened in horror at the sight, and she wrapped her arms around me in a hug.

"Sara, what happened?" she asked.

I shook my head. "I don't know. Madison, did you see anything unusual about Mr. Lee today? Did he say anything to you?"

"No, nothing. I didn't even realize he was still here. Everything seemed normal until... this."

"The ambulance and police should be here any minute," I told her.

We waited together, the minutes stretching endlessly, as customers slowly trickled out, their expressions a mix of curiosity and concern.

Finally, the sound of sirens pierced the tense atmosphere, and within moments, the bakery was a flurry of activity. Police officers and paramedics streamed in, cordoning off the area around Maxwell Lee.

"Ma'am, please step back," a stern voice commanded. My head snapped up to see two police officers approaching me.

"Hi, I'm Officer Taylor and this is Officer Lopez. Are you the manager of this bakery?" a tall man with graying hair asked.

"Yes, I am the owner of this bakery. I'm Sara Baker. Please call me Sara."

"Do you mind if we ask you some questions?" Officer Taylor asked.

"No problem. Should we talk in my office?" I suggested.

"That's a good idea," Officer Lopez nodded.

I led them to my small office in the back, a space filled with the clutter of baking orders and invoices.

"Sara, we need to understand Mr. Lee's activities in your bakery today," Officer Taylor began. "Did he consume any food here?"

I nodded, trying to keep my voice steady. "Yes, he had a slice of key lime pie. It's one of our specialties."

Officer Lopez pulled out a notepad and began jotting down notes.

"Did Mr. Lee express any discomfort or unusual reactions after eating the pie?"

"No, nothing like that. He did criticize the pie for being too sweet, but there were no signs of physical discomfort."

"When did Mr. Lee come into your bakery?"

"Around 11:30 in the morning."

"Do you know Mr. Lee well?"

"Not really. I only met him once before today in a social gathering."

"Did you notice anyone unusual or suspicious in the bakery during Mr. Lee's visit?"

I racked my brain, trying to remember. "No, it was just regular customers. I didn't notice anyone out of the ordinary."

The seriousness in Officer Taylor's eyes was evident as he asked, "Sara, do the key lime pies you serve contain any ingredients that might cause a severe allergic reaction?"

I paused for a moment. "No, Officer. I only use common ingredients in the key lime pies, ones that can be bought at any grocery store. There's nothing unusual in them."

"And these ingredients are?" Officer Lopez prodded, pen poised over her notebook.

"Standard baking items," I explained. "Flour, sugar, butter, eggs, and of course, key limes. Then there's the graham cracker crust which is just graham crackers, butter, and a bit of sugar. For the meringue topping, it's just egg whites and sugar. All pretty basic ingredients."

Officer Taylor nodded, while Officer Lopez jotted down notes. The air in the room felt thick.

"Have there been any incidents in the past where someone had an allergic reaction to your pies?" Officer Taylor asked.

"Never. We're very careful about food allergies here."

I could sense the officers weighing my words. The notion that something in my beloved pies could have contributed to Mr. Lee's death was distressing.

Officer Taylor's voice was somber as he spoke. "Sara, preliminary indications suggest Mr. Lee may have died from natural causes. However, at this stage, we cannot rule out the possibility of foul play. Because Mr. Lee died from unknown causes, an autopsy will be performed to determine the exact cause of his death."

My hands trembled slightly as I processed the implication of his statement.

"I understand," I managed to say.

Officer Taylor continued, "We'll need to interview other employees and perhaps some of the customers who were in the bakery today. It's standard procedure in situations like these."

I nodded. "Of course, whatever you need. My staff will cooperate fully. I'll make sure of it."

"Thank you, Sara. We may need to speak with you again as the investigation progresses," Officer Taylor said as he stood up. Officer Lopez, who had been quietly taking notes, followed suit.

As they left my office, heading toward the main area of the bakery to begin their interviews, I remained seated, trying to gather my thoughts.

The last of the flashing lights disappeared from outside the bakery, leaving behind a stillness that felt both eerie and heavy. The police had finished their initial investigation, and the medical team had transported Maxwell's body away for an autopsy.

I turned to Madison. "Maddy, let's close up early today. Go home and try to get some rest. We all need it."

"What about tomorrow, Sara?"

I sighed. "We won't open tomorrow. The police might need to come back for more questions, and honestly, I think we could all use a day to process this."

Madison and I began lowering the blinds and switching off the display lights. Once everything was shut down, I waved Madison goodbye and locked the doors from inside.

Exhausted and still reeling from the day's events, I retreated to the quiet sanctuary of my office. I needed advice, someone to guide me through the legal maze that I feared lay ahead. I reached for my phone and dialed Sophia, a well-respected lawyer.

"Sophia, it's Sara. Something terrible happened at the bakery this afternoon. Maxwell Lee, the food critic, he... he died here," I said, my voice shaky.

There was a sharp intake of breath on the other end. "Oh my God, Sara, are you okay? What happened?"

I quickly briefed her on the situation, my words spilling out in a torrent. When I finished, there was a brief silence as Sophia processed the information.

"First, Sara, I want you to take a deep breath. This is a serious situation, but you need to stay calm. The first piece of advice I can give you is not to make any public statements about Mr. Lee's death, especially to the media. Anything you say could be misconstrued or used against you."

I nodded, scribbling down her words.

"Second," she continued, "fully cooperate with the police investigation. Provide them with any information they request, but also be aware of your rights. You don't have to answer questions without a lawyer present if you don't want to."

"Should I hire a lawyer now?"

"It's a good idea to have legal representation, just to be on the safe side. I can recommend someone who specializes in this type of situation."

"Thank you, Sophia. This... this happened so fast."

"Sara, stay strong. This is a tough situation, but you'll get through it. And remember, I'm here for you."

After ending the call with Sophia, I set the phone down gently on my desk. I leaned back in my chair, feeling a wave of emotions crash over me. It was as if the floodgates had opened. Tears held back during the long, surreal day, began to flow freely. I buried my face in my hands, my body shaking with sobs. The image of Maxwell, lying lifeless in a corner of my bakery, flashed before my eyes, haunting me.

"Why? How could a day that started ordinarily end like this?" The unfairness of it all overwhelmed me.

I cried for what felt like hours, mourning the jarring intrusion of death into a place that represented life and joy.

Gradually, my tears subsided. Wiping my eyes, I stood up, knowing that I couldn't stay in the office forever, lost in my sorrow. I gathered my things, turned off the lights, and left the bakery.

Chapter 5

My hands trembled as I fumbled with the key to our house. When I managed to unlock the door and step inside, I was greeted by the smell of freshly brewed coffee and Tom's warm smile.

"Hey, Honey. How was your day at the bakery?"

"Where is Amanda?" I asked.

"She was waiting for you earlier. She is now taking a nap after dinner."

"Tom, something terrible has happened at the bakery today." My voice cracked under the weight of my emotions.

"Tell me everything," he urged, guiding me to the couch where we sat down together. Ginger silently hopped up onto the couch and curled up on my lap.

As I recounted the horrifying discovery of Maxwell's body, the arrival of the police, and their interview, tears welled up again in my eyes.

"The police have no idea what they're talking about," Tom snarled. "You would never hurt anyone, Sara."

"But, Tom, how do we deal with the situation?"

"Let's start by considering the possible causes of Maxwell's death. Could it be an allergic reaction? Was there anything with peanuts in the bakery today?"

"No, the key lime pies don't have peanuts, or any nut products for that matter. I'm always careful with allergens."

"What about a heart attack? After your argument, you said Maxwell's face turned red. That could be a sign, right?"

"I suppose it's possible," I admitted. "Our argument was heated, and he seemed quite upset. However, he was in his forties. If he did have a heart attack, he could have asked for help and everyone in the bakery would have come to his aid and called an ambulance. While I am no doctor, I can confidently say that he was fine when I left him and returned to the kitchen."

"Should we tell the police about the argument and his reaction?" Tom asked.

"I already did during the interview. Tom, if he died from a heart attack, could I be held responsible?"

"I'm not sure, Sara," Tom said slowly. "But remember, you have good insurance for the bakery. It's there to cover accidents and unforeseen events like this."

"What if that's not enough? What if his family blames me?"

"We'll hire a lawyer if it comes to that. But let's not jump to the worst-case scenario just yet. The autopsy results will shed more light on what happened."

"You're right," I said, trying to draw comfort from his logic. "It's just so hard to think straight with all this uncertainty."

"Could anyone at the bakery have wanted Maxwell Lee dead? Perhaps they witnessed your heated exchange with Maxwell and took it upon themselves to intervene?"

I looked at him, taken aback. The suggestion that someone from my bakery could harbor such malice seemed inconceivable. "No, Tom. I know everyone who works for me. They're like family. None of them would... could ever do something like that."

Tom's expression softened. "I'm sorry, Sara. I didn't mean to upset you. I'm trying to consider every possibility."

"Are you implying that Maddy might have been involved in this? But she wasn't even at the bakery when the argument took place." My voice grew louder, and I could feel my competitive nature trying to break through.

"Oh no, I didn't mean it like that. I know Maddy would never want to harm anyone," Tom said, and I could see regret flickering in his eyes.

"I understand you're trying to help," I said, struggling to keep my voice steady. "But they are good people, Tom. They're as shocked and saddened by this as we are."

He reached across the table, covering my hand with his. "You're right. I shouldn't have said that. I trust your judgment, and I know you care deeply for your staff. I love them, especially Maddy."

I nodded and we sat in silence. The gentle ticking of the kitchen clock was a reminder of time passing. That's when my phone beeped. I glanced at the screen to see a message from Madison. She had sent me a link to a newspaper article.

I tapped the link, and the headline filled the screen: "Breaking News: Famous Food Critic Dies in a Local Bakery." My heart sank as I began to read the article.

Key West Gazette
April 18, 2024
Breaking News: Famous Food Critic Dies in a Local Bakery
By Jonathan Hayes

In a shocking turn of events, renowned food critic Maxwell Lee was found dead this afternoon in "Sara's Sweets," a popular local bakery known for its delectable key lime pies.

Lee, famous for his sharp critiques and influential reviews, was visiting the bakery as part of his tour of Key West's culinary scene. The circumstances of his death are currently under investigation, with initial reports suggesting no obvious signs of foul play.

The local police department has stated that an autopsy will be conducted to determine the cause of death. Officer Taylor, one of the lead investigators, commented, "We are deeply saddened by this tragic event. Our thoughts are with Mr. Lee's family during this difficult time. We are exploring all possibilities and conducting a thorough investigation."

Lee's death has sent ripples through the culinary world, where his influence was both feared and revered. Locals and tourists alike frequented "Sara's Sweets" for its cozy ambiance and delicious treats, making this incident all the more shocking to the community.

Further details will be provided as the investigation progresses.

As I showed Tom the article, a hollow feeling settled in my stomach.

"I'm worried, Tom. What if this incident scares customers away and my bakery goes under because of all the negative attention? What if this is the end of my business?"

"That won't happen. Sara, you're tough, and your bakery is more than just a place. People love it for its warmth and the delicious treats you create. This... this is just a terrible incident. It will pass."

I wanted to believe him, but fear and doubt clouded my thoughts. As if sensing my distress, Ginger placed her head gently on my lap, looking up with those big, soulful eyes.

I stroked Ginger's soft fur. "It's just so unfair. One moment, everything is fine, and the next, everything I've worked for is under a shadow."

There seemed to be many steps I could take to try and save the bakery, but I had no idea where to even begin. I had never felt so powerless and confused about what to do.

Chapter 6

Wednesday

Early morning light began to filter through the curtains, casting a soft glow across the bedroom. Tom and I were still nestled in the comfort of our bed when the sound of the front doorbell pierced the quiet of the morning. Ginger's barking followed immediately.

Who could it be at this hour? I quickly slipped out of bed, threw on a robe, and hurried downstairs.

I opened the front door to find Officer Taylor and Officer Lopez standing on the doorstep, their police badges glinting in the morning light.

"Good morning, Sara. May we come in?" Officer Taylor asked.

"Of course," I replied. A wave of unease washed over me as I led them into the living room. Ginger quieted down but stayed close, her eyes following the officers.

"Is everything alright?" I asked as I tied the sash of my robe. Tom appeared at the top of the stairs, concern etched on his face as he quickly joined us.

As we sat in the living room, Officer Taylor said. "Sara, we need you to come down to the police station to answer some more questions about Mr. Maxwell Lee's death."

"Why? I answered your questions truthfully yesterday. What's happened?"

Officer Taylor exchanged a glance with Officer Lopez before turning back to me. "The initial autopsy results have come in. They indicate that Mr. Lee did not die of natural causes. This is now being treated as a homicide investigation."

My heart skipped a beat, and I felt Tom's grip on my hand tighten.

"How could it be a homicide? There was no blood, no sign of any struggle or injuries..."

"The initial autopsy results suggest that Mr. Lee was poisoned. There were no external signs of harm because the cause of death was internal."

Poisoned? The notion that someone could have intentionally harmed Mr. Lee, especially in my bakery, was terrifying.

"But how? Who would do such a thing?" I asked.

"We're working to find out," Officer Lopez responded. "However, the final toxicology report, which will give us more specifics about the poison, may take another week."

"Sara, I'm afraid you are currently our prime suspect," Officer Taylor said, his tone professional. "We need you to come with us to the station to answer some questions."

I felt as if the ground had opened up beneath me. "Me? Your prime suspect? But I didn't... I wouldn't..."

Tom's face flushed with anger as he stood up from the couch and took two steps toward Officer Taylor.

"This is ridiculous! You should be out there looking for the real killer instead of wasting time here accusing Sara of something she didn't do!"

Officer Taylor stood up from his chair and I could see his jaw tighten. "Mr. Baker, I understand this is upsetting, but we have procedures to follow. It's not a matter of accusing without reason. Some questions need answers."

"Procedures? What about accusing innocent people? What about catching the real killer?" Tom countered, his hands clenched at his sides.

I reached out, trying to calm Tom, but he was too agitated, his protective instincts fully roused.

It was Officer Lopez who stepped in, her voice calm. "Tom, we know you're a dedicated firefighter. You understand the importance of following protocols in a crisis. We're just doing our job, trying to piece together what happened."

Tom glanced at Officer Lopez, then back at Officer Taylor, his anger simmering just below the surface. "Sara is innocent. She would never harm anyone."

"We're not making any conclusions," Officer Taylor reassured. "There are things that I can't talk about outside the police station. We need Sara to come with us to clear up a few things. That's all."

Tom's shoulders slumped slightly. "I'm coming with you, Sara," he said firmly, his gaze meeting mine.

"No, Tom. I need you to call Sophia first. Ask her to meet me at the police station. She'll know what to do."

"OK. I'll meet you at the station as soon as I take care of everything here."

"Remember to send Amanda to daycare and go to work as usual. And please, stay calm. Let me handle this."

Tom gave me a reassuring hug. "We'll get through this."

As I walked out of the house, accompanied by the officers, I could feel the curious and shocked eyes of our neighbors upon me. The quiet suburban morning was disrupted by the sight of me entering the back of a police car. Whispers and murmurs floated through the air.

Sitting in the back of the police car, I felt a strange sense of detachment. This couldn't be happening. It was like a scene from one of the mystery novels I read, not my life.

Chapter 7

The interrogation room in the police station was stark, with a clinical feel to it. The walls were gray, and the only furniture was a plain table and a few chairs. A fluorescent light buzzed overhead, casting a sterile glow over everything. I sat in a hard-backed chair, as Officer Taylor and Officer Lopez sat across the table from me.

"Sara, we have eyewitnesses who saw you having a heated argument with Mr. Lee at your bakery yesterday morning," Officer Taylor began.

I nodded, my hands clasped tightly in front of me on the table. "Mr. Lee came to visit my bakery yesterday. We had an argument about the taste of my key lime pie."

Officer Lopez, who had been quietly observing, spoke up. "Can you tell us more about the nature of this argument?"

I took a deep breath. "Mr. Lee was criticizing my key lime pie, saying it was too sweet and lacked the proper tartness. I disagreed with him on the balance of flavors. It was purely a professional disagreement, about the pie."

The officers exchanged a glance. I continued, "I pride myself on my baking, and Mr. Lee's critique was harsh to me.

It was important for me to defend my work, but there was no malice in our exchange. It was just a difference of opinion."

I could feel their scrutinizing eyes on me, weighing my words. The room felt suffocating.

"Can you tell us the details of the key lime pie you served Mr. Lee? When was it baked, and where did you prepare his order?" Officer Taylor asked, his eyes fixed on me.

"The key lime pies were baked early in the morning, as part of our regular baking routine. When Mr. Lee arrived, I went back to the kitchen to cut a slice from a pie I had set aside for his visit."

Officer Lopez interjected, "Why not just serve a piece from the display case on the front counter?"

"I was expecting Mr. Lee's visit," I explained. "He was a well-known critic, and I wanted to present him with the best we had. So, I reserved the most presentable pie from that morning's batch specifically for him."

There was a brief pause before Officer Taylor leaned forward. "Did you add anything to that pie? Any poison, to silence Mr. Lee's negative opinion about your key lime pies?"

The accusation hit me like a physical blow. "No, absolutely not!" My voice rose in disbelief and hurt. "I would never do something like that. I take pride in my work, but hurting someone, especially in such a manner, is unthinkable to me."

Officer Taylor held my gaze for a moment longer before making a note.

"Sara, we're going to have to shut down your bakery until we can confirm it's safe to open for business."

"Is that necessary?" I protested. "The bakery is everything to me and my staff, and there's no reason to think it's not safe. How are we going to live without the bakery?"

"I understand this is difficult," Officer Taylor replied. "But given the circumstances, we need to ensure the safety of your customers. It's standard procedure in a situation like this."

As the reality of the situation sank in, I knew arguing wouldn't change the decision. "How long will it be closed?"

"We can't say for certain right now," Officer Lopez answered. "We'll conduct our investigation as quickly as possible."

I nodded, feeling a sense of resignation wash over me.

Officer Lopez leaned forward. "Sara, had you met Mr. Lee before yesterday?"

I cast my mind back. "We met once briefly at a social gathering for local business owners. We exchanged a few words about the community and local businesses."

Officer Taylor interjected. "Was Mr. Lee blackmailing you? Promising a good review of your key lime pies in exchange for something?"

The absurdity of the question took me by surprise. "Blackmail? No, of course not! Our interactions were professional. There was no such arrangement or conversation."

Before I could fully process the implication of his question, Officer Taylor asked. "Did you recently pay Mr. Lee

$10,000 in cash? We have access to Mr. Lee's financial records."

The question was like a bolt from the blue. "What? $10,000? No, I didn't pay him anything! Why would I? I don't know where you're getting this information, but it's completely false."

There was a moment of silence as Officer Taylor and Officer Lopez exchanged a knowing glance.

The door to the interrogation room swung open abruptly. Sophia, confidently poised and professional, strode in. Upon seeing her, I felt like a lifeline had been thrown to me in turbulent seas.

"Good morning, I'm Sophia Rodriguez, Sara's lawyer." Sophia turned her attention to Officer Taylor. "Are you charging my client with the murder of Mr. Lee?"

"No, we are not charging her at this moment."

Sophia nodded, then turned to me. "Sara, don't say another word. We're leaving."

I stood up, my legs feeling unsteady, and we walked out of the room together.

As Sophia and I approached the front door of the police station, Officer Lopez caught up to us.

"Sara, I just want to thank you for your cooperation today," she said, her voice tinged with a sincerity that hadn't been present earlier. "We are doing everything we can to catch whoever is responsible for Mr. Lee's death."

Her words, meant to be reassuring, instead opened a floodgate of emotions within me. Tears prickled at the corners of my eyes. I blinked rapidly, fighting the urge to succumb to the overwhelming desire to break down.

"I appreciate that, Officer," I managed to say. "Please, catch whoever is responsible."

Sophia placed a supportive hand on my shoulder. "Officer, we trust you'll conduct a thorough investigation."

With that, we stepped out of the police station, the sunlight harsh after the dimness of the building.

Chapter 8

I followed Sophia to her car.

"Sophia, where are we going?" I asked once we were both settled inside.

"We're going to 'The Cozy Corner.' Ava and Jennifer are waiting for us there. We thought you might need some friendly faces and a good meal."

"That sounds wonderful."

The moment we stepped into "The Cozy Corner," Ava and Jennifer rushed over to me. They enveloped me in a hug.

Sitting at our usual table by the window, I looked at my friends. "The police think someone poisoned Maxwell. And they're considering me their prime suspect."

"And I'm now officially her lawyer," Sophia added.

Shock and disbelief crossed Ava and Jennifer's faces. "That's absurd, Sara," Ava exclaimed. "You would never do something like that."

Jennifer reached across the table. "The police are barking up the wrong tree!"

"I know it sounds crazy. But that's what's happening. My bakery is being shut down for the investigation, and everything feels like it's falling apart."

"We're here for you, Sara, no matter what," Ava said.

Jennifer nodded in agreement. "We need to do something. We just need to figure out who could have poisoned Maxwell."

"So, who would want to hurt Maxwell?" I asked.

Ava was quick to respond, "What about his ex-wife? Weren't there rumors of a messy divorce?"

Jennifer took out her phone. "Let's make a list. We can start with personal connections like his ex-wife and then look into professional rivalries."

Sophia added, "We should also consider anyone who might have been negatively impacted by his reviews. A harsh critique from Maxwell could ruin a business."

We each took out our phones, diving into the depths of the internet. The search was a mix of social media deep dives, news articles about Maxwell's past reviews, and forums where his name was mentioned.

As we compiled names and possible motives, the reality of Lee's complex and contentious world became apparent. There were restaurant owners who had closed shops after scathing reviews, chefs who had publicly expressed their disdain for him, and several personal relationships that seemed strained and turbulent.

The list seemed endless. "This is like looking for a needle in a haystack," Jennifer remarked, her eyes scanning through another article.

Sophia nodded. "It's a complex web. But it's a start."

I sat back, feeling overwhelmed.

A thought suddenly occurred to me. "If Maxwell was poisoned, he must have ingested it before he came to my bakery. We should find out who he interacted with yesterday morning, or even the night before."

Ava's eyes lit up. "That's a great idea, Sara. Perhaps someone slips poison into his breakfast or coffee."

Jennifer said, "We could check his social media accounts. People often post about their meetings or check in at locations."

"And what about credit card statements? They could show where he was and who he might have been with. We'll need to get the police to look into that. I have contacts within the police department and I will see if they are open to sharing any information with me," Sophia added.

"I'm not going to sit on my hands while my bakery is shut down," I declared. "The police have so many cases, and this might not be their top priority. I'm going to start by paying a visit to Maxwell's ex-wife. Maybe she can shed some light on things."

Ava chimed in immediately, "I'll come with you, Sara. You shouldn't do this alone."

"Yeah, I'll join you. Just let me know beforehand when you plan on making these visits," Jennifer said.

"Thank you, but you all have busy lives," I smiled. "I think I can handle this. Besides, a one-on-one conversation might be more conducive to getting information."

Sophia looked at me. "Just be careful, Sara. You're delving into potentially sensitive territory."

"I will. I just need to start somewhere."

Chapter 9

I parked my car a few houses down from the home of Susan Miller, Maxwell Lee's ex-wife. I had no idea how she'd react to my questions.

"Okay, here goes nothing," I muttered as I got out of the car and approached the house.

The doorbell chimed softly as I pressed it. My heart raced, but I tried to keep a calm expression on my face.

"Can I help you?" A woman in her late 40s answered the door, her blond hair pulled back into a messy bun.

"Hi, I'm Sara Baker. I know this might be an odd request, but I was wondering if I could talk to you about your ex-husband, Maxwell Lee."

She hesitated for a moment before finally opening the door wider and allowing me to enter. "Alright, come in. Call me Susan."

"Thank you," I said, stepping inside the modest living room. I noticed an old family photo hanging on the wall, showing a younger version of Maxwell and Susan, along with a teenage girl who resembled him.

"Is that your daughter in the picture?" I asked, pointing to the photo.

"Emma? Yes, that's her. She's sixteen now. She hasn't seen Maxwell in years."

"Did she ever talk about her father?"

"Cut the small talk," Susan snapped, her eyes narrowing. "What do you want to know?"

"Sorry. I didn't mean to intrude. You know, Maxwell passed away while he was in my bakery and the authorities are suspecting foul play—they believe someone poisoned him. It's just... his death has left many questions unanswered, and I thought perhaps you might have some insight into his life. Maybe help me understand why someone would want to harm him."

"Understand? That man was a walking disaster, always leaving pain and misery in his wake. As for why someone would want to harm him, I can think of countless reasons."

"Would you mind sharing some of those reasons?"

"Maxwell was a cruel, heartless man, always looking for ways to belittle and demean those around him." Susan paused, her gaze distant as she delved into the past. "Our marriage was nothing more than a game to him, a way to assert his control and superiority."

"Did he ever hurt you?"

"Not physically. But emotionally? Oh, he was a master at that. He could make you feel worthless with just a glance, and he reveled in it."

"How did your marriage with him affect your life?"

"Everything I had, everything I was, revolved around him. It took me years to reclaim my own identity after our divorce." She stared hard at me. "He had a fondness for whores, and I'll never be able to forgive him for that."

Her words hung heavy in the air between us.

"He sounds like a real piece of work," I commented. "But still, that doesn't justify violence, does it?"

"Those who cause others pain should not be surprised when it eventually comes back to bite them."

I could feel the resentment radiating off her as she spoke. But did that mean she was involved in his demise? Susan didn't strike me as a killer.

"Thank you for your candor. I appreciate you taking the time to speak with me."

"Whatever," she replied, her voice dismissive. "Just make sure you find whoever did this."

"Do you have any ideas on who might have a grudge against Maxwell?"

"I haven't been involved in his life for quite some time, so I'm not aware of any recent beef he may have had. You should probably speak with his mother, she is always by his side."

"Can you give me her address?"

"I'll look it up for you." she scrolled through her phone before showing me the address. "Just don't mention to Lucy that I give you her address."

"I won't," I assured her, stepping back toward the door. "Goodbye."

"Goodbye." Susan shut the door firmly behind me.

Chapter 10

I approached the old house on the outskirts of town with determination in my step. The sun was beginning to set, casting a warm glow on the neatly trimmed hedges and the white picket fence that surrounded the property. As I knocked gently, I could hear shuffling noises from within. The door creaked open, revealing a stooped figure with wispy white hair.

"Hello, Mrs. Lee. My name is Sara Baker. I'm trying to find out what happened to your son, Maxwell. May I come in to talk to you?"

"Come in. Please, take a seat. The police were just here and they informed me that my son was murdered." Mrs. Lee motioned toward an antique armchair.

"Who are you and why are you here?"

"So sorry for your loss, Mrs. Lee. Your son passed away at my bakery. I'm doing everything I can to assist the police in finding the culprit."

"If I were younger, I would join you in your investigation, knocking on doors and searching for answers."

As I settled in, I couldn't help but notice a photo album lying on the coffee table. Its leather cover was worn and its pages were yellowed with age.

"Mrs. Lee, I spoke to your former daughter-in-law, Susan. She mentioned that her relationship with Maxwell was... strained. Could you tell me about your relationship with your son?"

"Maxie was always a proud man," Lucy began. "Ever since he was a boy, he insisted on doing things his way. It made him successful, yes, but it also pushed people away."

"Did you ever have any conflicts with him?"

"Every parent has disagreements with their children, but we loved each other. In recent months, he became more distant and more focused on his career. Sometimes, I felt like I hardly knew him anymore."

"Can you think of anyone who might have wanted to harm Maxwell?"

"Maxie made many enemies throughout his career," she admitted. "But I can't say for certain who would've gone to such a violent extreme."

"Mrs. Lee, may I take a look at this photo album?" I asked, gesturing toward the coffee table.

"Of course," she said, handing it to me with trembling hands.

I turned the pages. The images showed a much younger, happier Maxwell surrounded by his family and friends. He had an arm around Susan in some, while others featured him cradling his infant daughter, Emma.

"Is that Rachel Monroe?" I asked, pointing to a photograph of a young woman with fiery red hair.

"Yes," Lucy looked at the photograph and replied. "She and Maxie dated once, but they had a falling out years ago. I never did find out what happened between them."

"I know Rachel pretty well. She runs her own bakery now." I closed the album and handed it back to her.

"Please, you must find the monster who took my son's life," Lucy pleaded, her eyes filling with tears. "Maxie may not have been perfect, but he didn't deserve to die like that."

"I promise I'll do everything I can." I stood up to leave.

Mrs. Lee's memory was jogged by something sudden. "Oh, I just remembered, there is someone you should look into. His name is Jonathan Thorn. Maxie mentioned to me once that he got into a fist fight with him."

"Thank you, Mrs. Lee. You've been incredibly helpful."

Chapter 11

Jonathan Thorn, a well-known food critic in his own right, was a stark contrast to Maxwell in many ways. Where Maxwell was harsh and arrogant, Jonathan was more balanced and approachable. Locating his contact was not as hard as I'd feared. Thanks to a quick online search, I found his office address. I picked up my phone and dialed his number. "Hello, Mr. Thorn? This is Sara from Sara's Sweets..."

Surprisingly, he agreed to meet me.

As Tom and I sat in the elegantly decorated lobby of his office building the following day, I glanced at Tom. "You think he has anything to do with Maxwell's death?"

Tom shrugged. "Hard to say. But we're here to find out."

The moment we were ushered into Jonathan's office, I could tell he was a man who savored the finer things in life. The space was adorned with culinary awards and glossy food magazine covers.

A man in his early fifties with graying hair and spectacles, Jonathan sat behind a mahogany desk.

As we settled into the plush chairs, I began. "Mr. Thorn, I'm Sara, and this is my husband, Tom."

"Please, call me Jonathan. What brings you to my office?"

"We're trying to figure out what happened before Maxwell Lee died in my bakery."

"Ah, yes, the unfortunate incident at 'Sara's Sweets.' I read about it. Terrible business, truly."

Tom said. "We were hoping you might shed some light on Maxwell's last few days. Did you see him at any food events or gatherings recently?"

Jonathan stroked his chin thoughtfully. "Maxwell was quite the gastronome. We did cross paths at a few tastings. But to be honest, he kept to himself."

"Did he mention anything unusual, or anyone he was concerned about?" I pressed.

Jonathan hesitated. "There was this one evening at a gala. He seemed rather anxious, and kept looking over his shoulder."

"Jonathan, Maxwell's mother mentioned something about a fistfight between you two," I said, watching his face closely for any telltale reactions.

He let out a short laugh, rubbing the back of his neck. "Ah, that. It was a misunderstanding, blown out of proportion."

Tom leaned in. "A misunderstanding that led to a fistfight seems rather serious."

Jonathan sighed. "It was years ago. We were both at a prestigious culinary event. Tensions were high, and words were exchanged over a critique I wrote about one of

Maxwell's articles. Things escalated quickly, but it was nothing more than a momentary lapse of judgment."

"So, it was strictly a professional disagreement?" I asked.

"Absolutely. I respected Maxwell's talent, even if we didn't always see eye to eye."

I mulled over his words. "And after this incident, how were things between you two?"

Jonathan leaned back in his chair. "I see where this is going. Maxwell and I had our differences. But it was professional, not personal. I'm a food critic, not a murderer."

Tom cut in, "We understand that, Jonathan. But we have to look at all possibilities. You were in a public feud with him, after all."

"I can see why you'd think that. But at the time of his death, I was at the Gotham Culinary Conference in New York. I can provide you with the itinerary, plane tickets, hotel booking, everything."

"Can anyone vouch for your whereabouts?" I asked.

Jonathan nodded. "Of course. You can talk to anyone who attended. They'll tell you."

"Jonathan, do you know of anyone who might have wanted to harm Maxwell?" I asked.

Jonathan's face flickered with a shadow of unease. He clasped his hands together on the desk, drawing a long breath before speaking. "There were rumors," he said cautiously, "rumors that Maxwell engaged in... unsavory practices."

I leaned forward, my interest piqued. "Unsavory practices?"

He nodded. "Blackmail, to be precise. It was said that he used his influence as a critic to leverage favorable reviews from local restaurants. Quite the scandal, if true."

Tom raised an eyebrow. "Did you ever see any direct evidence of this blackmail?"

Jonathan shook his head. "No, nothing concrete. Just whispers in the culinary world. Chefs and restaurateurs speaking in hushed tones. But Maxwell was a powerful figure; few would dare to openly cross him."

"So, no one has ever come forward with proof?" I asked.

"Unfortunately, no. In our industry, reputation is everything. The fear of retribution, whether from Maxwell or the public, kept lips sealed."

"Thank you for taking the time to speak with us, Jonathan," I said.

As we stood to leave, Jonathan's eyes held a reflective glint. "Maxwell's passing was a shock to us all. He was a remarkable food critic. His loss is felt deeply in our community."

Stepping out of his office, I felt a chill despite the warmth of the day. The idea of Maxwell Lee wielding his critical pen like a sword over the heads of chefs and restaurant owners added a sinister twist to the investigation.

As we sat in the car, I turned to Tom. "When I was questioned at the police station, Officer Taylor asked if Maxwell had been blackmailing me. At the time, I didn't understand what he meant."

"Jonathan mentioned something about Maxwell blackmailing people with negative reviews."

"That's right. And Officer Taylor asked me if I had recently given Maxwell $10,000 in cash, which didn't make any sense to me at the time. But now it does."

"So, it seems that some people were blackmailed for $10,000 and one of them might have decided to poison Maxwell as a result. That could be a motive for murder," Tom suggested.

He turned to me with a look of deep concern. "Sara, I'm worried about how deep we're getting into this. Maxwell's murder... it's not just a simple mystery anymore."

"I know, Tom. It's becoming more complicated than I ever imagined."

"You shouldn't be going to interview these persons of interest alone. It's not safe."

"You're right."

Tom's brow furrowed as he stared through the windshield. "Maybe we should just step back and let the police handle the investigation. This is getting out of hand."

"Tom, I wish it were that simple. But with my bakery closed and my name being dragged through the mud, I don't see any other choice. The only way to clear my name as soon as possible is to continue digging."

Tom's expression softened. "I just don't want anything to happen to you, Sara."

"I know," I replied, squeezing his hand. "And I promise I'll be careful."

Tom drove us back home and I quickly pulled up the website for the Gotham Culinary Conference. Jonathan Thorn was listed as one of the speakers at the conference. So, indeed, he was in New York on the day Maxwell was murdered.

Chapter 12

The moment Tom and I opened the front door, the comforting scent of home enveloped us. Amanda bounded toward us while Madison emerged from the kitchen with a dish towel slung over her shoulder. Ginger was close on their heels, her tail wagging.

"Mommy, Daddy, you're back!" Amanda exclaimed, throwing her arms around us in a tight embrace.

Madison smiled. "Dinner's almost ready. I hope you're hungry."

The aroma of pesto chicken wafted through the air. "It smells amazing, Maddy. Thank you for taking care of dinner," I said.

Madison served the pesto chicken, its rich, herby scent mingling with the homely smell of baked potatoes.

As we sat around the dinner table, Madison turned to me with a concerned expression. "So, how did the investigation go today?"

I sighed, my fork hovering over my plate. "We're hitting a wall, Maddy. It's like every step forward leads us two steps back."

Tom reached over and gave my hand a reassuring squeeze. "We just need to keep digging and stay patient."

"Mom and Dad called me earlier. They're really worried about you, Sara, and about the bakery," Madison said.

I felt a lump form in my throat. "I know. But it's not just about the bakery anymore; it's about clearing my name and finding out the truth."

After dinner, as the clinking of dishes faded into the background, Madison and I found ourselves alone in the quiet of the living room.

"Sara, what's the next step for the bakery?"

"We have to wait until the police finish their investigation of Maxwell's death. Until then, our hands are tied."

Madison frowned. "I've been hearing things, Sara. Rumors around town. It seems like someone is intentionally spreading nasty talk about 'Sara's Sweets.'"

"Who is spreading these rumors?"

"I don't know. It's just so unfair. You've worked so hard to build a reputation for your bakery. It's heartbreaking to see someone trying to tear it down with baseless gossip."

I felt a mix of anger. "I know. This whole situation is complicated. Right now, it's difficult to determine who exactly we are dealing with. But once the police and we uncover the person responsible for Maxwell's death, all these speculations and rumors will disappear."

"I'm counting on you, Queen Bee."

"How are Antonio and Janet doing?"

Madison sighed. "They're frustrated, understandably. But they're hanging in there."

"I hate that they're caught up in this mess."

"I'm worried about the bakery, Sara. The lost sales... it's going to be tough."

"We will be fine. I had saved up to open a second location. But now, I'll use that saving to keep our current bakery afloat."

"That's a big sacrifice, Sara."

"This is a curve ball, but we'll get through it. With time, our name will be cleared, and 'Sara's Sweets' will be back to glory."

Chapter 13

The sun cast long shadows on the sidewalk as I approached Rachel Monroe's bakery. Meeting Rachel was never an easy feat, especially given our history.

Rachel and I had opened our bakeries within weeks of each other, five years ago. At first, our relationship was cordial, the kind of friendly rivalry you'd expect in a small town. But as the years passed, the competition grew more fierce.

I remembered the first incident that marked the beginning of our rivalry. It was a summer festival, and both our bakeries had entered the pie contest. I was confident in my key lime pie, but Rachel's cherry pie won the judges' hearts. I couldn't deny that her pie was good, but the way she flaunted her victory, the smug smile as she lifted the trophy, had left a bitter taste in my mouth.

From then on, our rivalry escalated. When I introduced sourdough bread, Rachel came out with a multigrain loaf that she claimed was healthier and tastier. When I started offering gluten-free options, Rachel countered with a vegan line. Our rivalry was competitive in a way that kept me on my toes.

"Welcome to 'Tropical Treats'!" a young employee said behind the counter.

"Is Rachel around?"

"Yes, she is! Just a moment." He disappeared into the back.

Rachel emerged from the back, her red hair pulled into a tight bun, sharp features accentuating her piercing green eyes. She wore a clean white apron, not a single speck of flour or icing marring its surface.

"Good afternoon, Sara."

"Hello, Rachel. Could we have a little chat?"

"Of course," she replied, gesturing toward a small table in the corner.

"Your bakery is doing well," I said, as we sat down.

"I heard the police shut down your bakery. Are you here to look for a job?"

"No, Rachel, I'm not looking for a job. My bakery is temporarily closed while the police investigate the death of Mr. Maxwell Lee. He was quite the influential food critic."

"Maxwell Lee was a cruel man. We could all use a break from his heartless critiques."

"He said my key lime pies were too sugary."

"I can't blame him for thinking that." Rachel wasted no time in taking a jab at me.

"I believe it's just a matter of personal taste. Did Maxwell have anything positive to say about your bakery?" I attempted to steer the conversation in a different direction.

"Thankfully, he didn't get the chance to try it," Rachel replied with an odd smile, her gaze fixed on the ceiling.

"I heard that you knew him quite well."

"Who told you that?"

"Maxwell's mother showed me a photo of you two together. She mentioned that you had a falling out. Care to fill me in?"

"Maxwell and I dated once, but that was a long time ago. We argued over many things," she admitted, her jaw tightening. "He could become violent if he didn't get his way. But that's all in the past now."

"Were you in touch with him at all before his death?" I asked.

Rachel hesitated for a moment before responding. "No, not really. I haven't had a conversation with him in the last few months."

"I'm just trying to find out what happened to him. He didn't deserve to die like that."

"I understand. He died in your bakery, after all," Rachel said, her voice icy. "Now, if you'll excuse me, I have a bakery to run."

"Of course. Thank you for your time, Rachel."

As I left the bakery, I couldn't help but wonder whether Rachel was hiding something more. Her connection to Maxwell was undeniable, but the question remained: how deep did it go?

Chapter 14

I kissed Amanda's forehead, her curls bouncing as she giggled and scampered off to join the other kids at the daycare. As I turned to leave, my phone buzzed.

"Hey Sara, it's Ava," came the chirpy voice on the other end.

"Good morning, Ava. What's up?"

"Listen, I just heard something wild," Ava said. "Maxwell Lee..."

My grip on the phone tightened. "What about him?"

"He was seeing Ruby LaRoux, from the strip club on Fifth."

I leaned against the wall for support, feeling the texture of the wallpaper press into my back. Maxwell Lee and Ruby LaRoux? If he was with Ruby the night before he died...

"Are you there, Sara?"

"Yeah, sorry, just processing. That's quite the bombshell."

"Right? And I thought, what if Ruby knows something that could help clear your name?"

"You're thinking we should go talk to her?"

"Exactly! Maybe she saw or heard something important."

"Okay, let's do it. When?"

"Tonight. I'll meet you outside the club at 8. Wear something... not bakery-ish."

"Got it. Thanks, Ava. I owe you one."

"Girl, you owe me a dozen key lime pies after this."

"Deal. See you tonight."

The neon sign buzzed overhead, casting a lurid glow on the cracked pavement as I pulled up outside the strip club. My hands trembled slightly on the steering wheel. With a deep breath to steady my nerves, I stepped out into the night.

I scanned the crowd for Ava's face. The evening air was thick with the scent of cheap perfume and cigarette smoke. It wasn't long before I spotted her near the entrance, her dark hair cascading over her shoulders, contrasting against her vibrant red dress.

Ava caught my gaze, and her lips curled into a smile. Together, we approached the bouncer, a mountain of a man whose stern expression softened just a touch at the sight of Ava.

"Evening, ladies," he grunted, stepping aside to let us pass.

As we crossed the threshold, the dim lighting swallowed us whole.

"Ready?" Ava whispered, her hand briefly squeezing my arm.

"Let's find Ruby."

The bass vibrated through the soles of my shoes, climbing up my legs and seizing my chest in a rhythmic clench. Lights, red and blue, flickered like the wings of tropical birds. My gaze struggled to adjust as Ava led the way.

"Over there!" she shouted over the music. "By the stage!"

I followed her pointing finger. We wormed our way through the crowd, each patron a blurred face, an anonymous body swaying and undulating to the hypnotic pulse of the music.

When we reached the edge of the stage, the lights converged into a single, stark spotlight, and there she was—Ruby LaRoux. Her dance defied the limits of what seemed impossible for the human body. Every twist and turn of her body was in harmony with the pulsing rhythm of the club's music. The shimmering fabric of her costume caught the light, casting prisms on the walls like scattered jewels.

"What are we even going to say to her?" I muttered.

Ava leaned close. "We'll start with hello. And then... we ask about Maxwell."

I watched Ruby's performance reach its crescendo. The men's eyes were fixated on her contorted body. Some extended their hands over the stage, pressing dollar bills underneath her pink bra.

The final notes of Ruby's song faded, and the crowd erupted into cheers and whistles. She gave a sultry bow. As people clamored for more, she turned and disappeared behind the heavy velvet curtains.

"Come on." Ava gripped my arm.

We slipped past a burly bouncer, who was too busy eyeballing a rowdy patron. Backstage was a labyrinth of dimly lit corridors. Our heels clicked against the concrete floor.

Ava nudged me, and I turned to see Ruby at the end of the hallway. She was peeling off long, sequined gloves, as she headed toward what I assumed was her dressing room.

"Ruby LaRoux?" Ava called out.

Ruby stopped in her tracks, her posture stiffening before she slowly pivoted to face us. Her makeup was bold and dramatic, her hair a cascade of fiery curls that framed her sharp features.

"Can we talk to you for a minute?" I asked.

She assessed us with a wary expression. "Who are you?"

"I'm Sara Baker, and this is Ava Patel. We just have a few questions about Maxwell Lee."

Recognition flickered across Ruby's face, and she took an involuntary step backward, her heel catching on a coil of cable. Ava reached out to steady her, but Ruby regained her balance with a dancer's grace.

"Maxie?" There was a tremor in her voice. "Why do you want to talk about him?"

"Please, it's important. We just need a few minutes of your time," I said.

Her eyes searched mine, and for a moment, I thought she might turn away. But then, with a sigh, she nodded.

"Alright," Ruby motioned toward a door marked "Private." "Let's talk."

We filed into the cramped space behind the door, the air thick with the scent of heavy perfume and stale smoke. Ruby perched on a worn-out chair, legs crossed.

"Ruby," I began. "I want to know about what happened to Maxwell Lee in his last days."

Her dark eyes flickered, darting to Ava before settling back on me

"Maxie died several days ago." She swallowed hard, her fingers fidgeting with the fringe on her costume. "What do you still want to know about him?"

"Your relationship," I pressed, watching her face for any twitch, any telltale sign that might reveal more than her words would.

She hesitated, biting her lower lip. It was as if she was weighing her next words. "It's none of your business."

"Please, Ruby," Ava pleaded. "It's not easy for us to come in here. We are trying to uncover the truth behind Maxwell's death. Any information you can give us would be greatly appreciated."

"We were... close," Ruby finally admitted. "Occasionally, he would come to the club to pick me up after I finished dancing and drive me back to his house or my place. The last time I saw him was the night before... before he passed away." Her voice cracked on the last word, and she quickly added, "I miss him. A lot."

It struck me as ironic that out of all the individuals I had conversed with about Maxwell, it seemed that the one who missed him the most was a stripper. I gave her a sympathetic nod to show my understanding.

I clasped my hands in front of me. "Was Maxwell okay that night? Healthy?"

"He was fine that night," she said, her voice steady. "Maxie was full of life—like always. Strong as a tiger."

"Any signs of illness? Anything out of the ordinary?"

"Nothing. If there had been, I would've noticed. He left my place in good spirits the next morning."

A piece of the puzzle had just fallen into place with an almost audible click. If Maxwell had been healthy leaving Ruby's embrace, then his poisoning must have occurred shortly after, before he came to my bakery—the timeline was narrowing.

"Thank you, Ruby." I quickly slipped a $100 bill into her hand and rushed out of the room with Ava in tow.

Outside the club, the neon glow from the club's sign cast a surreal sheen over us, throwing our shadows against the wall.

"Did you see her face?" Ava whispered. "She didn't even try to hide it."

"Because it's the truth. Maxwell was poisoned after he left Ruby... which means..."

Ava's brow furrowed as she spoke, "So he was poisoned that morning before he entered your bakery...Where do we go from here?"

"I'm not sure. It's getting late, so let's head back home. I'll mull it over tomorrow. Tom must be worried sick by now. It was a struggle to convince him not to come with me."

"And maybe we should talk to the police again. With this new piece of info..."

"Maybe. They've probably talked to Ruby already."

The strip club's door swung open behind us, spilling laughter and music into the alley.

"OK. Goodnight, Sara."

"Goodnight, Ava." I watched her drive away before walking to my car.

Chapter 15

The salty breeze tousled my hair as we reached the shoreline of Key West Beach. Tom, with that boyish grin he saves for days off, unloaded our cooler and umbrella from the back of the car while Amanda hopped around like a little sandpiper. Ginger's tail swept back and forth as she watched every move we made.

"Can we go to the water now, Mommy?"

"Just let me put down this towel, sweetie." I spread out our family's claimed territory.

Tom drove the umbrella into the sand with a few expert twists. He stood up, wiped his hands on his shorts, and cast a satisfied look over our setup. "Looks like base camp is ready."

"Yay!" Amanda squealed, grabbing Ginger's leash from my hand. "Come on, Ginger! Race you to the waves!"

The sky was a canvas of azure, painted with only a few wisps of white. The ocean stretched out like a vast, sparkling jewel, its surface winking at me. Palm trees swayed gently, their fronds casting dancing shadows on the warm sand.

"Beautiful day, isn't it?" Tom stood beside me, his arm finding its way around my waist.

"Perfect." I leaned into his solid frame.

"Last one in's a rotten egg!" Amanda's voice carried back to us.

Ginger barked in agreement, matching the spirit of our little girl who was already knee-deep in the gentle surf, splashing and laughing as the waves welcomed her in.

"Look at this spot," I said, pointing to a pristine stretch of beach near the water's edge. "Perfect for sandcastles."

Tom grinned. Amanda clapped her hands as she plopped down onto the warm sand. Ginger settled beside her, head tilted.

"Let's make it a fortress," Amanda's imagination already ran wild. "With towers and a moat!"

"Your wish is my command, princess." Tom began to dig a wide circle around our construction area.

I scooped up a handful of moist sand, feeling its grainy texture between my fingers. We filled buckets, flipped them over, and tapped them out to form the base of our castle. Ginger seemed more interested in digging her holes than appreciating our architectural efforts.

"Mom, make the bridge here!" Amanda pointed, and I obliged, carving a delicate archway with the edge of a plastic shovel.

"Looks sturdy enough for a king's arrival," I said.

"Or a queen's!"

"You are right."

After a while, the castle stood complete with turrets reaching toward the sky and a deep moat encircling it. We all stepped back to admire our handiwork.

"Time to defend the kingdom from sea monsters!" Tom announced, scooping up a colorful beach ball.

"Monsters don't stand a chance against us!" Amanda cheered, jumping to her feet.

"Ready, Ginger?" I called to our four-legged companion, who was already in position, tail wagging ferociously in anticipation. Tom threw the ball high into the air, and like a furry missile, Ginger launched after it.

"Good catch!" Amanda praised as Ginger returned, dropping the ball at our feet with a proud look in her eyes.

"My turn!" Amanda took the throw this time, sending the ball toward the ocean. Ginger raced after it, agile and swift, before it even had the chance to land. She returned, her coat speckled with wet sand, and the game continued.

"Nice throw, Sara!" Tom complimented me when it was my turn again, the ball sailing through a perfect arc into Ginger's eager leap.

As I shook the sand from our beach blanket, a high-pitched squeal from Amanda cut through the salty air. "Ice cream! Look, they've got ice cream!" Her little hand tugged insistently at mine.

"Can I have ice cream, Mommy? Please?" she pleaded, bouncing on the balls of her feet as she pointed to the colorful vendor cart stationed just a few yards away.

Tom caught my eye over her head. "Looks like someone's got her heart set on a treat."

"Well, how can we say no to that face?"

"Yay! Thank you, Mommy!"

"Come on then, let's go get that ice cream," Tom announced, ruffling Amanda's curly hair as we made our way to the vendor.

"Strawberry for me!" Amanda declared.

"Make that three strawberries, and... do you have key lime?" I asked the vendor.

"Sure do, fresh batch made this morning." he scooped generous portions onto sugar cones.

"Perfect. Two strawberries and one key lime," I said, accepting the tangy green swirl with a nod of thanks. "It's 'research,'" I joked to Tom.

"Of course, Honey. Very important research," he played along, taking his strawberry cone and leaning down to sneak a quick kiss on my cheek.

"Mommy, look at Ginger!" Amanda's laughter rang out, and I turned just in time to see Ginger inching closer to her cone, her nose twitching with interest.

"Ginger, you can't eat ice cream," I said, leading the way back to our towels.

We settled down, the sweet taste of ice cream perfect contrast to the salt on my lips. I nestled into the forgiving embrace of our striped beach towel, the grains of sand beneath conforming to my body like a natural cushion. The sun was tender in its warmth, lavishing my skin with a gentle heat that felt almost therapeutic. Here, under the vast expanse of a cloudless sky, I could feel the coiled tension begin to unfurl.

"Look at her soar, Mommy!" Amanda's voice pulled my gaze toward the shoreline where she and Tom took turns guiding a kaleidoscope kite through the sea breeze. It danced in the air, vibrant against the clear blue sky.

"Higher, Daddy, higher!" Amanda cheered, and Tom obliged, sending the kite swooping upward on an invisible current.

"Beautiful, isn't it?" he called over his shoulder.

"Absolutely," I replied, though I wasn't just talking about the kite.

As I soaked in the serenity, my thoughts began to drift, back to the puzzle that had consumed me. I picked at the fringe of the towel, my mind piecing together the fragments of information we'd gathered so far. Where had Maxwell taken his first sips of coffee that morning? Who had seen him? Witnesses were key, and I needed to find them.

"Tom!" I called out. He turned from the kite, passing the string to Amanda.

"Everything okay?" Tom's brow furrowed as he made his way back to me.

"We need to figure out where Maxwell ate breakfast that morning."

Tom nodded, understanding flashing in his eyes. "You think that's where the next clue is?"

"At breakfast, someone might have noticed something... off. Or maybe he met with someone."

"Okay." Tom brushed sand from his hands. "How do we find out where he ate the breakfast?"

"That is the question." I squeezed his hand.

"Okay, team, let's pack it up," Tom said, casting a glance at the setting sun.

"Right." I looked over at Amanda who was now chasing Ginger along the water's edge.

"Come on, Manda, Ginger! Time to pack up!"

"Five more minutes, Daddy?"

"Make it quick," Tom chuckled, and I couldn't help but smile at his soft spot for our daughter.

Chapter 16

I rounded the corner onto Main Street, the familiar sight of my bakery springing into view. My heart jumped at the sight of the yellow tape wrapped around the front door. "Police Line—Do Not Cross" screamed silently at me. I stopped by the bakery to collect the mail that had accumulated over the past few days.

"Hey, Sara!" Mr. Peterson from the florist waved. "Real shocker about Maxwell, huh? You holding up okay?"

"Doing my best, Mr. Peterson."

"Let me know if you need anything, dear," he said before retreating into his shop.

I made my way down the narrow alley, and soon enough, the backdoor appeared before me. I reached into my pocket and retrieved the key, its familiar cool metal resting against my fingertips. The key slid into the lock with a satisfying click, and I nudged the door open.

I stepped across the threshold. With the door shut behind me, I allowed myself a moment to breathe in the solitude before setting off on my search for the mail.

The air clung to me like an unwanted shroud, thick with the scent of sugar left to sour and flour gone stale.

"Come on, Sara," I muttered to myself, shaking off the eerie stillness that hung over the room like cobwebs.

I navigated between stainless steel tables—a landscape so familiar, yet now foreign in its deserted state. There it was, that secluded nook by the cookbooks and dog-eared mystery novels, where Maxwell had last drawn breath. My gaze swept over the area, searching. Could the police have missed something? A thread, a scrap, a clue they'd overlooked in their scrutiny?

My hands roved across the spines of books, dipped into the shadows behind stacks of parchment paper, and traced the edges where the wall met the floor.

"Maxwell, what brought you to this spot?" I spoke as if he could answer.

I knelt closer, and that's when a glint of white caught my eye. Wedged between the oak of the bookshelf and the floor was a small folded piece of paper. Its edges just barely peeked out from the darkened corner.

I reached for it, my fingers grazing the cool surface. "What is this?" I murmured, coaxing the paper free from its hiding spot. A surge of adrenaline rushed through me as I unfolded it.

The header read "The Spicy Pepper" in bold letters. Below, itemized neatly, was an array of breakfast options with one circled: "Huevos Rancheros—extra jalapeños."

"Breakfast order..." I whispered to myself, studying the time stamp. It dated the morning of his death. Could it be a coincidence? Or something more telling?

I tucked the paper into my pocket, feeling the outline of the receipt press against my thigh.

"The Spicy Pepper," the little diner just a few blocks away, was a place Tom and I frequented for comfort food. It could also be where Maxwell started his last day.

"Time to stir the pot," I declared.

Chapter 17

I could see the "The Spicy Pepper" in the near distance, its bold red awning flapping gently in the breeze. I quickened my pace, thinking about the receipt.

Pushing open the door, the rich aroma of spices greeted me. Maria stood behind the counter, her smile inviting.

"¡Sara! Qué sorpresa!" She hurried from behind the counter, her arms outstretched. "What brings you here today? Don't tell me you've finally decided to trade in your whisk for some chili peppers!"

I returned her embrace. "Not quite, Maria. I wish it were under happier circumstances."

Maria's brow furrowed. "Is everything okay, querida? Is Maxwell Lee's incident in your bakery still bothering you?"

"Actually, I could use your help."

She glanced around the now-quiet restaurant before gesturing me toward a secluded booth at the back. "Let's sit down. Tell me what's going on."

We slid into the booth, the vinyl squeaking softly beneath us.

"Maria, Maxwell visited my bakery last Tuesday morning before... before his death. I need to find out where he was before that—anything that might explain his health state when he came to visit my bakery."

"Of course, Sara. How can I help?"

"I have a feeling Maxwell might have stopped by here for breakfast that morning. Did you happen to see him?"

"Nothing comes to mind immediately," Maria replied. "I could have been in my office rather than at the counter."

I reached into my pocket and pulled out the crumpled receipt, smoothing it out against the surface of the table before sliding it toward Maria. Her eyes locked onto the faded print as I explained, "I find this receipt near the location where Maxwell's body was found. He must have dropped it in my bakery. This receipt could be a crucial piece in understanding his last hours."

"This is a receipt from my restaurant, dated last Tuesday."

"Can you check if he was here? It's important."

"Let me see what I can find." Maria stood up and disappeared behind the counter.

Moments later, she returned, a tablet clutched in her hands. Her finger traced line after line on the tablet screen until it stopped abruptly. "Here it is. Maxwell Lee, 8:15 am, table seven. He ordered the huevos rancheros, water... and he paid with his card. Look." She turned the tablet around, pointing at the entry.

"So Maxwell did eat breakfast here," I breathed out, relief mingling with fresh unease. "Maria, do you have any security camera footage from that morning?"

"Yes, we have cameras. They're for everyone's safety. Let's go take a look."

She led me through the restaurant and we arrived at a door marked "Private." Maria fished out a set of keys from her pocket, unlocked it, and ushered me into her office. The room smelled faintly of spices, and papers were stacked neatly on the desk alongside a small monitor connected to the security system.

"Here we go," Maria said as she booted up the system. She clicked through various screens until a grainy image of the dining area appeared, timestamped with last Tuesday morning.

"Can we start around 8:00 am? Just before he came into the restaurant."

"Sure thing." Maria's fingers flew over the keyboard as she adjusted the time settings.

The screen flickered and then stabilized, showing the early breakfast crowd. My eyes were glued to the monitor, scanning for Maxwell's distinctive figure. Time seemed to slow down as we watched customers come and go, waitstaff weaving between tables with plates of food and refilling coffee cups.

"Pause!" I said suddenly. "There... table seven."

Maria hit the space bar, freezing the frame. We leaned in, scrutinizing every pixel of Maxwell as he sat alone, his posture upright and his attention occupied by his meal.

"Let's see when he leaves," Maria murmured, resuming the playback.

"Wait! Go back a bit," I said, as something on the edge of the screen caught my eye—a shadow, a movement. But upon closer inspection, it was just another customer passing by.

"It appears that he had a peaceful meal alone. Anything else you want to see?" Maria asked after a while.

"Let's watch until he leaves. Just to be sure."

On the screen, Maxwell appeared self-absorbed. He kept his eyes focused on his plate, only lifting them briefly to glance at the menu resting next to his elbow.

"Huevos rancheros," I recalled Maria's description of his order earlier. "He doesn't look like he's expecting anyone."

"And no one appears to be watching him either. It seems… ordinary."

"I was hoping to find a clue to the cause of his death." My voice trailed off, disappointment settling over me like a heavy apron. I had hoped for a suspicious character lurking nearby or an exchange of secretive gestures—anything that could point me toward answers.

"Something happened after his breakfast, Sara."

"Let's continue playing," I said and we watched in silence. With each bite of his eggs, and each sip of water, my hope deflated further. Finally, the scene shifted; Maxwell glanced at his watch, laid down some bills on the table, and stood up. The clock on the camera feed marked 9:30 am when he exited the frame.

9:30 am—an entire hour unaccounted for between this relaxed departure and his arrival at my bakery.

"Is there anything else I can help you with?"

I shook my head slowly, my mind now racing to fill that sixty-minute void with scenarios and possibilities that might explain where Maxwell went after he left The Spicy Pepper. Who had he met? Did he have an appointment, or was it a chance encounter gone awry?

"Thank you so much, Maria. You've been more helpful than you know."

"Anything for you, Sara. You know you're like family here."

Chapter 18

I stood in the baking aisle, my gaze fixed on the shelf before me, debating whether to grab the premium vanilla extract or stick with the store brand. The shrill ring of my phone cut through the hum of the grocery store.

"Hello?" I answered.

"Sara! It's Helen! Your deck... it's on fire!" My neighbor's voice was laced with panic.

My heart thudded against my ribcage. "Fire? Are you sure?"

"Yes! I'm looking right at it! Flames and smoke, Sara. Where are you?"

"I'm at the grocery store. I'll be right back." I fumbled to end the call.

I immediately dialed Tom, who was having another 24-hour shift. The phone rang once, twice, and then his voice came through.

"Hey, babe. Everything alright?" Tom asked, likely envisioning a query about dinner plans.

My voice shook as I spoke. "Tom, it's our backyard... Helen just called. The deck is on fire."

"Fire? Oh no," Tom's casual tone disappeared.

"Tom, can you come home right now? I was grocery shopping but now I am going back home. Ginger is still inside the house."

"Of course, I'll make emergency calls and head home immediately. Stay away from the fire, Sara. We'll be there as soon as possible."

I burst through the sliding doors of the grocery store. The half-filled shopping cart was abandoned in my wake. A tin of baking powder rolled off the edge, but I didn't look back.

"Ma'am, you can't leave—" someone called after me, but their voice drowned in the thunderous beat of my heart.

I threw myself into the car and quickly inserted the keys into the ignition, twisting them to start the engine. I threw the car into reverse. Tires squealed against the pavement as I sped out of the parking lot. Houses and storefronts blurred past.

"Deck on fire? How did that happen?" I shook my head.

The turn onto my street was too sharp, the tires crying out in protest as I hugged the curb. The car skidded to a halt in the driveway, and through the windshield, a nightmarish sight unfolded before me.

Thick plumes of smoke billowed into the clear afternoon sky. Our deck, once the stage for family barbecues and lazy Sunday mornings, was now a monstrous bonfire, flames licking hungrily at the edges.

I killed the engine and jumped out of the car. The scent of burning wood stung my nostrils and clouded my vision. My breath came in sharp gasps, as I sprinted toward the house. I opened the garage door, grabbed the garden hose, and brought it out.

The sound of sirens grew louder, slicing through the thickening air, and I turned to see Tom's firetruck skidding around the corner. The bright red engine ground to a halt, its lights a frenetic dance of red and white.

"Tom!" My voice was lost in the chaos, but he saw me.

"Hi, Honey. Thankfully, only the deck is on fire, not the whole house. We'll have the fire under control shortly."

"Ginger is still inside the house. Should I let her out of the house?"

"No, it's safer for her to stay inside."

Tom quickly shifted into action mode and barked orders to his team, "Get the hose ready!" They unraveled hoses with a speed that spoke of countless drills.

"Pressure's up!" came the call, and the first jet of water arced through the air, a silver ribbon against the smoldering orange. Tom manned the nozzle, his stance wide, bracing against the force that sought to push back.

"Keep it steady," he shouted.

"Watch the backdraft!" One firefighter warned, and they adjusted their approach, coordinating their efforts to attack the blaze from multiple angles.

"More water!" Tom called out, and the hose surged with renewed vigor. Steam rose in great clouds as water met fire.

I stood rooted to the spot. The heat from the flames brushed against my skin in angry waves, but I barely felt it.

The sound of a siren announced new arrivals, and I turned to see Officer Taylor and Officer Lopez stepping out of their patrol car.

"Sara, are you okay? Is anyone else inside?" Officer Taylor asked.

"I'm OK. Amanda is at daycare. My dog is still in the house, but I think it's best to leave her there for now."

Officer Lopez asked, "Do you have any idea what could have started the fire?"

"No, I have no clue. I was grocery shopping when the fire started."

Officer Taylor looked at the smoke billowing from the deck and asked, "Do you keep a propane tank on your deck?"

"No. Tom stores our propane tank in a shed away from the house. It couldn't have caused this fire."

"Is there any chance you have security cameras installed? Particularly any facing the backyard?" Officer Lopez asked, her notebook already in hand, ready to record every detail.

"Yes, we do. There's one that overlooks the deck."

"Will you be able to access the footage right now?" Officer Taylor asked.

"Yes, I can." I fumbled with my phone, barely able to punch in the security app's password. Officer Taylor and Officer Lopez leaned in.

"Here we go," I said as the live feed switched to the recording. The footage rolled back to reveal the deck, serene in the afternoon light, before it all changed.

My breath caught as a figure emerged on the screen, clad in dark clothing, face obscured by a ski mask. "There," I pointed. The dark figure moved quickly across our backyard.

"Look like a man," Officer Taylor stated.

"I agree," Officer Lopez added. "Likely a young male based on his movements. What's that he's got there in his right hand?"

"Looks like...a canister?" Officer Taylor suggested.

The man on the screen tilted the can, and even through the digital rendering, we could see the glint of liquid cascading onto the wood of the deck.

"God," I breathed out. "He's pouring it everywhere."

The man took out a cigarette lighter. The small flame seemed insignificant until it met the drenched deck, erupting into a hungry beast that consumed everything.

"That's clear intent. This wasn't an accident," Officer Taylor broke the silence, his jaw set in a hard line.

"Definitely arson," Officer Lopez agreed.

"Sara, could you recognize the person even if their face is concealed?" Officer Taylor asked.

"I don't know anyone with such an appearance."

The last of the smoke curled up against the darkening sky. Officer Taylor's hand rested on his belt. "Sara, I want you to know we're taking this very seriously. Arson is a grave offense, and we'll use every resource at our disposal to find who's responsible."

"I know you will, Officer." A part of me wanted to crumble, to let out all the fear and shock in one long, wailing cry.

Officer Lopez stepped closer. "We will check all the CCTV camera footage on this street. We will find the arsonist, Sara. And you did the right thing, getting us that video so fast."

"Please keep us posted," I said, meeting her gaze. "And I have more footage if you need—different angles, times..."

"Please send those over to us as well," Officer Taylor said, his walkie-talkie crackling once more and calling him back to duty.

"I certainly will."

"Stay safe," Officer Taylor said as he walked away.

"Call me if you need any help," Officer Lopez reached out her hand and I gripped it tightly before letting go.

Hoses coiled and helmets tucked under arms, the firefighters wound down their urgent dance around our charred deck. The crisp scent of spent embers tinged the air as I stepped closer to the wreckage, the deck now a blackened skeleton.

"We were lucky, Sara. The fire didn't spread to the main structure," Tom said, his face smeared with soot as he stripped off his heavy gloves.

"Lucky isn't the word I'd use right now." I watched as his team wrapped up.

"Everyone's safe, that's what matters," Tom said, reaching out to brush a stray ash from my hair.

"Could have been worse," I murmured, but the 'what ifs' gnawed at me. What if it hadn't been just the deck? What if I'd been home, oblivious, upstairs in the bedroom?

"Hey." Tom's voice pulled me back from the edge of those spiraling thoughts. "You're shaking. Let's get you inside, okay?"

Tom wrapped an arm around my shoulders and guided me toward our home. In the distance, I heard engines starting and saw the red truck preparing to leave, their job here done.

Chapter 19

I collapsed onto the couch, my face hidden within the refuge of my palms. The fabric beneath me felt cool against my skin, as tears cascaded down my cheeks.

"Sara, how are you doing?" Tom's voice cracked. "There is no need to worry."

I took a deep breath before speaking, my voice shaking. "Tom, I'm sorry for putting you, Amanda, and Ginger in danger. I feel like everything around me is falling apart lately. It's like I'm cursed or something."

"Hey, it's okay. Sometimes bad things just happen."

Just then, a warm tongue brushed against my hand, and a soft whine reached my ears. Ginger nudged her nose into my palm.

"Hey, girl," I said.

I thought about my bakery, the recent events, Maxwell's death, and my being a prime suspect. "But why? Why set our house on fire?"

Tom wrapped his arm around me. "It's too coincidental with everything going on at the bakery. Someone might be trying to intimidate us, maybe even silence us."

"If this has anything to do with Maxwell's death, it means we're getting closer to the truth and someone is trying to stop us from uncovering it," I reasoned.

"Sara, we need to change our approach. We have to stay lowkey and cooperate with the police. I don't want you or Amanda getting hurt."

Lifting my gaze to meet Tom's, I could see the worry written all over his face. My vision blurred as fresh tears threatened to fall from my puffy eyes. "The investigation's hit a wall anyway, Tom. I don't know where to go from here. And now... now I've put us all in danger."

"Don't put too much pressure on yourself. We'll figure this out. For the damage to the deck, I think the insurance will cover it."

I leaned into his chest, and gradually, the tempest inside me quieted to a drizzle. The last of my sobs ebbed into shuddering inhales and exhales. "We can't turn back now. No prisoners."

"Come on. Let me make you a cup of tea," Tom said softly, his hands supporting my elbows as he coaxed me upright. My legs felt rubbery, but Tom's steadiness anchored me as we made our way to the kitchen.

The familiar clink of ceramic and the soft swoosh of water filled the kettle were comforting sounds.

"Here," he said, turning around with a steaming mug cradled in his hands. I wrapped my fingers around the warmth, feeling the heat seep into my palms.

I took a cautious sip, the liquid a soothing trail of heat down my throat, steam curling up to brush my face. It was just how I liked it, a hint of honey sweetening the robust flavor.

"You are a good husband, Tom," I said and placed the mug on the table. Stepping closer, I pressed my lips against his.

"I need this," I murmured.

Tom responded eagerly, his breath mingling with mine as our mouths moved in sync. My heart raced as I melted into his embrace. His hand trailed down to my buttock, gently caressing it and drawing a moan from my throat. I cupped his face in my hands and deepened the kiss, feeling his arousal harden against me. "Sara," he whispered.

With a tight embrace that left me breathless, Tom lifted me off the floor and carried me to our bed.

Chapter 20

The clink of my spoon against the ceramic bowl mingled with the chirping of the early morning birds outside our kitchen window. I was halfway through a bowl of granola and yogurt when my phone rang. My heart leaped into my throat as I saw Officer Taylor's name flash across the caller ID.

"Hello?"

"Good morning, Sara. It's Officer Taylor."

"Good morning, Officer."

"I'm calling with some good news. The Police Department and the Health Department have wrapped up our investigation at your bakery."

I held my breath, the spoon I had been using now forgotten in my hand.

"We've given it the all-clear. You can reopen your bakery anytime you're ready."

A wave of relief washed over me so powerfully that I nearly dropped the phone. "Oh, thank God," I exhaled. "That's great news, Officer."

"Of course, Sara. We're just glad we could sort this out quickly. Take care, Sara. And if you need anything, don't hesitate to call."

"Officer Taylor, before you go," I blurted out. "Has the toxicology report for Maxwell Lee come in yet?"

There was a brief pause on the line. "Yes, Sara, we did get the results back. Maxwell Lee died from a rare poison."

"A rare poison? Can you tell me more about it?"

"Well, it's not something we see often. It's a plant-derived alkaloid. Very potent and not easy to come by. It acted slowly, which provided whoever did this with an alibi."

My fingers tightened around the phone. A slow poison? One that could throw off the timing and shield a killer? Who in our small town would possess the knowledge, let alone the intent, to execute such a plan?

"Thank you, Officer Taylor, for sharing this information."

"Sara, the forensic team didn't find any poison in your bakery."

"Sir, I wish you catch whoever did this as soon as possible. Let me know if I can be of any assistance."

"Appreciate that, Sara. We will keep in touch."

"Have a good day, Officer."

"Likewise."

As the call ended, I sat there for a moment longer. Then, I sprang into action.

I grabbed my phone, thumbing through my contacts until Madison's name appeared.

"Maddy, it's me," I said as soon as she picked up. "The bakery got the all-clear. We can open again."

"Really? That's great news, Sara!"
"Can you come help me clean up and prep?"
"Of course, sis. I'll be right over."
"See you in the bakery."
"See ya!"

A grin spread across my face as I hung up the phone. With my keys in hand, I swung open the door and stepped out into the refreshing morning breeze.

Chapter 21

I was about to enter "Sara's Sweets," when I saw Mr. Peterson shuffling up the cobblestone path.

"Morning, Sara."

"Good morning, Mr. Peterson. How are you? We've been given the all-clear to reopen. I'm looking forward to getting these ovens fired up again."

"That's great! Can't wait to taste your key lime pies again. The entire town has been craving your sweets since you closed for the investigation."

I chuckled. "Well, they won't have to wait much longer. We're reopening soon."

"Excellent news!" He clapped his hands together, then paused as something seemed to cross his mind. "Sara, did I ever tell you about the time I ran into Maxwell Lee on the morning he—"

"Passed away?" I completed his sentence with a softness in my tone. Mr. Peterson nodded gravely.

"Yes, yes. It was quite odd. He was gripping this large cup of coffee, his hand trembling slightly. And he seemed... uncomfortable."

"He was holding a large cup of coffee before he entered my bakery?"

"Indeed. He kept shifting it from hand to hand like it was scalding him through the cardboard. And he took off so quickly after our chat, almost spilling it."

"Thank you for sharing this with me. Have a great day, Mr. Peterson."

"You too, Sara." He continued down the street.

"Could the coffee cup still be around?" I mumbled to myself, calculating waste collection schedules against the timeline of Maxwell's last day.

I pushed open the door to my bakery, and the scent of sugar and cinnamon hung dormant in the air. Inside, Madison was already at work, her hair swept into a no-nonsense ponytail as she scrubbed down the counters.

"Hey, Sara." She glanced up.

"Good work, Maddy," I said, my gaze drifting over the immaculate display cases and polished floors. "But now there's something else we need to focus on."

"What is it?" She set down her sponge and straightened up.

"We need to find the trash bag from the day Maxwell died. Mr. Peterson just told me that Maxwell held a large coffee cup before he entered our bakery. The coffee cup could tell us a lot more about what happened."

She blinked, but then her expression evolved into one of understanding. "I see. Because of the shutdown, we didn't take out the trash. Therefore, that bag of garbage should still be in the dumpster out back."

"Great." I pulled on a pair of latex gloves, offering another pair to her. "Let's see if we can find the large coffee cup."

"Got it." Madison snapped the gloves tightly around her wrists.

We hurried through the kitchen toward the back alley where the dumpster stood like a silent sentinel.

"Here." I pointed to a black bag that was tied up neatly, sitting on top of two other trash bags. "That must be the one from last Tuesday."

"Let's hope no one's had a chance to add to it," Madison said.

"Okay, careful now," I said as we lifted the heavy bag between us and gently set it down away from the others. "We don't want to miss anything."

Our gloved hands plunged into the trash bag, stirring up a mélange of smells. The tang of citrus clung to crushed pastries, and the pungent sting of coffee grounds mingled with the faint scent of vanilla extract that had somehow found its way into the garbage.

"Ugh, this is worse than I thought," Madison grimaced, her nose crinkling as she withdrew a gooey mass of dough from the pile.

"Keep going. The cup has to be here somewhere." I tried to ignore the slick sensation of day-old frosting as it smeared across my fingers.

We delved deeper, the contents of the bag spreading out before us like the aftermath of some confectionery catastrophe.

"Here's a coffee cup... no, this one is from our store," Madison said, discarding a plain white styrofoam cup.

"Keep looking."

"Wait, what's this?" Madison paused, holding up a napkin stained with a vibrant smudge of lipstick.

"As far as I know, Maxwell didn't wear lipstick that day."

Madison winked at me. "You said when he came in, he seemed off?"

"That's what Mr. Peterson just told me. I was too anxious about his opinion on our key lime pies, so I didn't realize he was feeling uncomfortable that morning."

"Here!" Madison's sharp intake of breath drew my attention. Her hand hovered over a semi-crushed large coffee cup. The lid was askew, revealing a dark residue inside. "Is that—"

"Let me see." My chest was pounding with nervousness as I reached for the cup. This coffee cup was certainly not from our bakery. The logo of the cup was partially obscured by a paper napkin, but enough was visible.

"Careful, Sara, don't touch—It may contain the poison."

"I know." I steadied my trembling hands and gently extracted the cup from the rest of the trash.

"Is it...?"

I peeled back a corner of the stained paper napkin that clung to the cup. The bold script of "Tropical Treats" stood out like a beacon against the white cardboard background. It's the logo of Rachel Monroe's bakery.

"Maddy, look at this."

Her eyes widened as she took in the sight, then met mine with an understanding that needed no words.

"Wow, Sara, this is huge! If this cup was indeed the last thing Maxwell drank from, it could change everything."

I nodded. "This could be a key evidence."

"Let me grab a zip bag," Madison said, already on her feet, moving toward the supply closet.

I held the cup at the edge, mindful of the prints that might grace its surface.

"Put the cup in the bag!" Madison returned with a clear zip bag large enough to encase the oversized cup. She held the bag open.

"Here we go." I slipped the cup into the plastic bag, sealing it with a firm snap.

"Take this straight to Officer Taylor, immediately," I said, handing over the sealed bag. "Tell him the coffee cup was used by Maxwell Lee and needs to be tested."

"You are not going to hand it to Officer Taylor yourself?"

"I have a visit to make to Rachel Monroe's bakery."

"Got it, boss." Madison grasped the bag firmly.

I watched her leave and sat quietly for a moment. Everything that had happened in the past eight days clicked into place. My entire body trembled with the realization of how close I was to uncovering the truth. The urge to clear my name and seek justice burned within me and I knew it was time to take action.

Chapter 22

I pushed open the door to Rachel Monroe's bakery. My heart hammered against my ribs with the force of a battering ram.

"Welcome to Tropical Treats," Rachel called out from behind the counter, not yet looking up from her meticulous frosting of a chocolate cake.

"Rachel," I said, my voice cutting through the cozy hum of her shop like a knife. Her eyes snapped up to meet mine.

"Ah, Sara Baker, to what do I owe the displeasure?" Rachel asked as she set down the frosting spatula, her voice laced with sarcasm.

"Cut the act, Rachel. We both know why I'm here. Poisoning Maxwell Lee? Setting my deck on fire? I want answers, and I want them now."

The clatter of a customer setting a coffee cup on a table punctuated the silence that followed. Rachel's face was a mask, but her eyes betrayed her; they flickered away before settling back on me, hard and calculating.

"Accusations require evidence, Sara. And you're in no position to demand anything." Her tone was icy as she leaned forward slightly.

"This is about justice, Rachel. For Maxwell, for me, for everyone you've hurt with your actions."

"I don't know what you're talking about, Sara. You think I had something to do with Maxwell's death?" Rachel's voice was a high-pitched attempt at innocence, but her eyes darted from the display case to the door and back again as if looking for an escape.

"Stop lying, Rachel. You put poison into Maxwell's coffee last Tuesday morning."

Her laugh was hollow, forced. "You have nothing on me. Just baseless claims."

"Baseless?" I challenged. "I know Maxwell stopped by your bakery for coffee before coming to mine. He was holding a large cup with your logo on it. We found that cup, Rachel. It's game over for you."

The color drained from Rachel's face.

"Let me see the cup," she demanded, her lips pressing into a thin line.

"I sent the cup to the police for analysis. In the cup, they'll find the poison you used to murder Maxwell."

"Poison?" The word seemed to catch in her throat.

"Yes, Rachel. And once they confirm what I already know..." I let the implication hang in the air between us.

A shudder ran through Rachel's slender frame, her hands gripping the edge of the counter. "You don't understand," she whispered, her voice quivering.

"Understand what?"

"Maxwell... he was going to destroy me." Her eyes met mine, pleading for a shred of mercy. "He was going to publish a scathing review—said my pastries were 'glorified cardboard' and my coffee was barely fit for rats. I couldn't let him do that."

"Even so, it was not justified for you to kill him. You could've found another way."

"Another way?" Rachel scoffed, a bitter laugh escaping her lips. "I gave him $10,000 to hold his tongue, Sara. Ten thousand! And still, he would have his pound of flesh. My bakery would've been over."

"Rachel, poisoning him?" I shook my head. "You knew he'd go to my bakery next. You set me up to take the fall."

"Maxwell was cruel, vindictive." She wiped at a traitorous tear that escaped onto her pale cheek. "Had I known any other way to stop him..."

"By killing him? There's always a choice. And you made yours. Now it's time to face the consequences."

"I was cornered, Sara! Cornered by a man who held my fate between his callous fingers."

Rachel slumped against the counter, her red hair falling like a curtain to hide her face.

I looked at Rachel with a furrowed brow. "Did you set fire to my deck?"

She responded quickly, "No, I didn't. But you have a habit of prying into others' businesses."

I squared my shoulders, preparing to walk away from the wreckage of our conversation. But as I turned toward the door, Rachel's fingers latched onto my hand with an urgency that stopped me cold.

"Wait," Rachel hissed, her eyes glinting like flint. "You can't just—"

"Let go of me," I said. Her grip was tight, and for a fleeting moment, I wondered if the desperation I had seen could morph into something darker. Could she lash out at me too? My heart raced, every instinct screaming that I needed to get out of there.

"Bitch." The word scraped from her throat. Her nails dug into my skin.

"Rachel—" I began, but the sharp clang of the bakery bell cut me off.

"Rachel Monroe?" Officer Taylor's firm voice filled the quaint space as he strode through the door, with Officer Lopez close on his heels.

"Officers," Rachel stammered, releasing me at once. I stepped back, rubbing at the red marks her fingers had left.

"We have reason to believe you may be involved in Maxwell Lee's death. We would like you to come to the station to answer a few questions," Officer Lopez stated.

"Based on what? Hearsay?" Rachel snapped, her gaze darting between the officers and me. "You have absolutely no solid evidence against me! I'm not going to the police station without my lawyer."

My fingers itched around the edges of my phone, hidden within the pocket of my apron. I pulled the phone out, pressing my thumb against the screen to wake it up. "I have more than just hearsay."

The blood drained from Rachel's face at the sight of my phone, her eyes widening with the realization of what I did.

"During our little chat earlier, I recorded everything. Your confession is clear. You poisoned Maxwell's coffee because he threatened your business."

"Give me that!" Rachel lunged forward, but Officer Taylor was quicker, stepping between us with a hand extended to halt her advance.

"Easy now," he warned.

Officer Lopez approached me, extending her hand. "May we?"

"Of course." I handed over the phone.

"We'll need to verify this recording," Officer Lopez said, tucking my phone into a plastic evidence bag. Her eyes met mine, offering a silent nod of gratitude.

The metallic click of handcuffs closed around Rachel's wrists, sealing her fate. As the officers turned to usher Rachel toward the door, I felt a wave of emotions crash over me. But among them, one stood out clear and strong: triumph.

Chapter 23

I pulled the last batch of key lime pies from the oven, the aroma enveloping me in a warm, citrusy embrace. Each pie was a little masterpiece, the crust golden brown and buttery, baked to a perfect crispness. The key lime filling sat nestled in its flaky shell, its tangy scent mingling with the sweetness in the air.

I set them on the cooling rack and took a moment to garnish each pie with a dollop of freshly whipped cream. A sprinkle of lime zest on top provided a final touch of color and a hint of citrus aroma.

The scent of fresh pastry swirled around me as I placed the key lime pies on the gleaming display. Madison rushed over holding a tray of macarons.

"Where do you want these, Sara?" she panted, her cheeks flushed from the morning's frenzy.

"Front and center, Maddy," I replied, flashing her a grin.

"Mommy!" I turned to see Amanda bolting toward me, her curly hair bouncing with every step. Tom was right behind her.

"Careful, sweet pea," I cautioned, but it was too late. Amanda was already wrapped around my legs. I looked down to see Ginger sat on my foot, her tail wagging.

"Everything looks amazing, Honey." Tom planted a kiss on my forehead.

I leaned into his embrace for a long moment.

"Let's get ready to open those doors," Madison called out, clapping her hands for attention.

"Let's do this," I said. With all three of my employees at the ready, the grand reopening of "Sara's Sweets" would be as sweet as the treats we served.

The chime above the door heralded a steady stream of customers as the golden morning light bathed the bakery in a warm glow. I watched as familiar faces drifted in, their eyes surveying the display case.

"Good morning, Mrs. Henderson," I greeted one of our regulars. "The usual for you?"

"Of course, dear. I wouldn't miss your grand reopening for anything!"

Chuckling at her enthusiasm, I packaged a key lime pie and slid it across the counter.

"Looks like the whole town couldn't wait to get a taste of our key lime pie again," Madison commented from beside me, her hands expertly boxing up a dozen assorted macarons.

I had been stirring batter and arranging pastries since dawn, but the fatigue melted away when Ava, Jennifer, and Sophia walked in.

"I hope you haven't forgotten how to bake during your little hiatus," Ava teased, a playful glint in her eye as she handed me a bottle of champagne.

"Forgetting how to bake would be like you forgetting how to be sarcastic," I shot back with a smirk, taking the bottle.

Jennifer chuckled and interjected, "Well, everything looks divine, Sara."

Sophia nodded in agreement. "It's like stepping into a dream. A sweet dream."

The pop of the champagne cork punctuated the moment. We poured the bubbly liquid into flutes, the light from the morning sun catching in the effervescent swirls.

"To new beginnings and sweet success!" I toasted, raising my glass. The others joined in, their glasses chiming against mine.

But then, the front door swung open once more. Officer Taylor and Officer Lopez stepped inside.

The room fell silent. My pulse quickened, a familiar unease settling in my gut. Why would they come here, today of all days?

"Morning, Sara," Officer Taylor called out, striding toward the counter.

"Officers, what brings you here?" I asked. It wasn't lost on me that the last time they'd walked through that door, it hadn't been to sample my baked goods.

"Sorry to interrupt, just need a quick word, if you don't mind," Officer Taylor glanced around. My fingers tightened around the edge of the counter.

"Of course, let's step into the kitchen for some privacy," I motioned toward the back.

"Lead the way," Officer Lopez said.

The door to the kitchen swung shut behind us, muffling the hum of conversation from the bakery.

"Firstly, Sara," Officer Taylor began, his hat in hand—a gesture of respect that surprised me. "We owe you an apology."

I blinked, trying to process his words. "An apology?"

"Yes." He cleared his throat. "We were wrong to suspect you in Maxwell Lee's murder. It was a hasty judgment, and I'm sincerely sorry for the trouble it caused. You have every right to be upset with us."

"Sir, you were just doing your job," I managed to say, though my voice trembled slightly.

Officer Taylor nodded, glancing at Officer Lopez before turning back to me. "There's more news, and it's good. We've made an arrest in regards to the arson on your property—the incident targeting your deck."

"Who did it?"

"James Monroe, Rachel Monroe's brother. After thorough investigation, we uncovered evidence of his motive and involvement."

"James? But why?"

"Misguided loyalty to his sister. But rest assured, he'll face justice."

"Thank you, Officers, for all your hard work." Relief flooded through me, washing away the remnants of fear and suspicion.

"We're glad we could bring you some peace of mind," Officer Lopez said, a warm smile reaching her eyes.

"Officers, let's get back out there and celebrate."

"Yes, ma'am," Officer Taylor replied, tipping his hat once more as we stepped out of the kitchen.

Tom wrapped an arm around my shoulder and asked, "Any news, Honey?"

I grinned widely. "Yes, the police arrested James Monroe for setting fire to our deck."

The hushed voices rose into a chorus of cheers. Even Mr. Peterson, who rarely showed emotion behind his bushy white beard, was grinning from ear to ear.

"Three cheers for Sara!" someone called out, and the response was immediate and enthusiastic. "Hip, hip, hooray!"

"Everyone," I called out, "I can't tell you how much your support has meant to me these past couple of weeks. As a token of my appreciation, today, everyone gets a slice of our key lime pie on the house!"

The room erupted once more, louder than before. The cheer mingled with the clatter of plates and the ring of the cash register. I knew, without a doubt, we were going to be just fine.

www.ingramcontent.com/pod-product-compliance
Lightning Source LLC
LaVergne TN
LVHW041711060526
838201LV00043B/670